Reborn In Blue

M.J Knight

Copyright © 2020 by M.J Knight

All rights reserved. No part of this book may be reproduced or used in any manner without written permission of the copyright owner except for the use of quotations in a book review. For more information, address:
MjKnightauthor@gmail.com

FIRST EDITION

The unauthorized reproduction or distribution of a copyrighted work is illegal. Criminal copyright infringement, including infringement without monetary gain, is investigated by the FBI and is punishable by fines and federal imprisonment. Please purchase only authorized electronic editions and do not participate in, or encourage, the electronic piracy of copyrighted materials. Your support of the author's rights is appreciated. This book is a work of fiction. Names, characters, places, brands, and incidents are the products of the author's imagination or used fictitiously. Any resemblance to actual events, locales or persons, living or dead, is entirely coincidental.

Copyright @ 2020 M.J Knight
First publication: June 22nd, 2020
Cover art: M.J Knight
Editing: Mollie Barragan, Paula Smith
Formatting: M.J Knight
All rights reserved. Except for use in any review, the reproduction or utilization of this work, in whole or in part, in any form by any electronic, mechanical or other means now known or hereafter invented, is forbidden without the written permission of the publisher.
Published by M.J Knight

DEDICATION

I have so many people to thank, and this book is dedicated to all of them. So, I'm going to start at the beginning...

My mom and dad. They have been gone a combined 19 years, but the time I did have with them molded me into who I am today. They believed in me and pushed me to do whatever I wanted in life. They also gave me plenty of stories to tell.

Next, I want to thank my husband for putting up with my ranting and raving. For taking care of 5 kids after coming home from working all day to give me time to write. He has been my champion through all of this.

The next person I want to thank is someone I've never met. Mollie Barragan is the kindest most supportive person I have ever known. She is also an amazing editor, and the best sounding board. I don't think this book would have made it without her. She started off as a stranger and turned into an awesome friend. She also brought in a bunch of awesome beta readers that helped develop my book into what it is now.

Paula Smith. My sista from anotha mista! Thank you for believing in me and pining for the guys before anyone even knew their names. You are the original reader, and the first person I trusted with my idea. Me and you. Margaritas and pizza- June 22nd!

Annamarie, Jacqueline, Ashley, Hope. Y'all are the real MVPs. The feedback and support pushed me through when I was unsure if I should keep going. I love y'all!

To the authors: M.J Marstens, Crystal Ash, Katie May, Kathryn Moon and A.J Macey. Y'all's books inspired me long before the thought of writing bloomed in my brain. Without women like y'all to talk to, and look up to, I would have never even given a second thought to writing my own book. Y'all are rock stars!

Thank you finally to my Facebook group members and friends. For doing my silly polls and laughing with me at memes. Playing the games and participating in takeovers. I hope y'all enjoy my book baby. It's my heart in ink and I have never been so happy to have finger cramps!

Laissez le bon temps rouler!

Let the good times roll!

CONTENTS

Author Note..ix

Prologue 1

Chapter One: Ayida 6

Chapter Two: Holder 14

Chapter Three: Ayida... 29

Chapter Four: Fletcher 45

Chapter Five: Clint 58

Chapter Six: Ayida... 67

Chapter Seven: Clint 80

Chapter Eight: Holder 90

Chapter Nine: Cole 99

Chapter Ten: Ayida 108

Chapter Eleven: Fletcher 129

Chapter Twelve: Ayida.. 141

Chapter Thirteen: Cole 152

Chapter Fourteen: Ayida 159

Chapter Fifteen: Clint 165

Chapter Sixteen: Clint... 174

Chapter Seventeen: Holder 184

Chapter Eighteen: Ayida 196

Chapter Nineteen: Ayida 201

Chapter Twenty: Fletcher 221

Chapter Twenty-One: Ayida 230

Chapter Twenty-Two: Cole 243

Chapter Twenty-Three: Fletcher 252

Chapter Twenty-Four: Ayida...................................... 263

Chapter Twenty-Five: Holder..................................... 286

Chapter Twenty-Six: Ayida... 300

Chapter Twenty-Seven: Holder 312

Chapter Twenty-Eight: Ayida..................................... 317

Chapter Twenty-Nine: Clint 339

Chapter Thirty: Ayida... 348

Epilogue 378

Soundtrack.. 390

About the Author... 394

Author Note

This book is written in informal language to make the character's more appropriate for their everyday speech. There will be slang, swearing, and purposely misspelled words to help phonetically set the tone of the storyteller.

If you spot an error or typo that you feel should be corrected, that does not fit the tongue /person's style and manner of speaking, please do not report this to Amazon. I am happy to look into potential corrections if you would care to drop me a quick email at: MjKnightauthor@gmail.com

Prologue

The feeling of the wooden pole cracking his soft back, had me giggling in pure joy. The asshole had tortured me for half a decade, and I was over being scared. Have you ever been so mad at someone you imagine using the Jaws of Life on their actual jaws? Ripping their skull off and using it as an ashtray for your after-sex cigarette with a man that can actually give a real orgasm... *Just me?*

I was a woman possessed after being pushed into doors and dressers and having phones and half-empty beer bottles thrown at my head... I couldn't stop swinging that pole if God himself stood in front of me and said to. He would just have to look on in envy. I was getting my pound of flesh from this fucktard one way or another.

So, there he lays, drunk and high after a few days on a bender. Going in and out of consciousness, either from lack of sleep or the drugs leaving his system. My sorry excuse for an ex. We had been together since I was eighteen ... five long years.

It wasn't bad in the beginning. He was older, and I thought he was more mature. It didn't take long for the drinking and drug use to become an issue. I would try to leave, and he would cry. He needed me. He was sorry. He would do better.

Then came the other women. I would soon become emotionally numb to that after the first few times I got pushed down on the floor for asking questions. Later it became normal to be held hostage in a bathroom or closet if I tried to leave or disagreed with him. I cooked his meal in a way he didn't like. That deserved a drink in my face. I questioned where he was going? Got me locked in the closet for a few hours.

One day, five years after my hell on Earth started, he came in drunk, a common occurrence with him. Walking was almost impossible, much less putting up a fight. He fell on the bed, demanding food and sex. That was the last straw. It was like my psyche just snapped, and it wasn't me anymore... It was the crazy-ass, blood-seeking woman I knew I had to be. I found the wooden pole that he was going to use to prop the air conditioner up in the window. *If you didn't know, some people live in trailers where the air conditioner is in the window and held up with a pole. That way, the whole window doesn't come crashing down on the air conditioner. Those things are expensive as fuck!* It was long and sturdy with little give. It was like the best present I'd ever received. A sign from the universe that his time had come.

So, I just did what everyone wanted to do. I

didn't kill him, but I'm sure he wished he were dead. I beat every single inch of him till he was nothing but a purple splotch on the bed. I didn't stop till the pole broke. He was lucky I didn't shove that stick right up his small dicked ass. Then, I grabbed the handful of clothes I was allowed to wear, got in the hatchback, rolled down the windows, and drove till the sun came up...

That's how I got here. I'm starting over, but not somewhere new. I'm going back to where it all started and where my next life will begin.

Chapter One: Ayida

Stepping up on the porch of the old Victorian-style house is like stepping right back into my childhood. I haven't been home in five years. Mom passed away six years ago. I didn't want to come back here, but where else do I have to go?

I steady my nerves and knock on the heavy door. I hear the shuffling and muffled words right before it swings open. Bright green eyes now sit in heavy wrinkles. He has aged hard.

"You sure have changed. You gonna come in or just stand there, letting the cold out?" That's my dad, straight to the point. Ex-Navy SEAL and still lives by the code. The smell of starched shirts and menthol cigarettes rush back to me like an old friend.

My mom had been my best friend. My only friend. When she died, it put so much pressure on Dad, and he tried to step up. It wasn't his fault he didn't know about teenage girls or children in general. He was in his 70s when Momma passed. He did the best he could, but I was a wayward teen anyway. It didn't take me long to run when he got his new "friend" to help around the house barely a year after.

So here I am now. "Hey, Dad. How is the RV business going?" My dad might be ex-Navy, but he could sell ice in the Arctic. It's not that he is nice or even friendly looking. The man is scarier than anything Freddy Krueger could come up with.

"It's going. Why ya asking? Writing a book?" Aww, he is being so sweet, definitely going better than I thought it would.

"Nope, just wondering. How about Trish? She still stealing checks and gambling away her disability checks?" That earns me a chuckle. Said chuckle about knocks me over in astonishment.

"Hell, if I know. Haven't seen that nasty cunt in

a few years." He still cusses like a sailor, I see.

"Well, what are you here for? I know it's not just to see my pretty face. Did you finally grow a pair and leave that shit head? What's his name again?"

"Robert, Dad, and yeah I left him alright. Left him beaten and bleeding in the bed." Without any warning, I get a slap on the shoulder.

"There is that Underhill blood coming out! I knew it would eventually. So, was he breathing when you left, or did you finish him the way your Old Man would?"

Did I mention my dad had also been in prison? Nothing violent, just money laundering for the Mob in the 70s. His violent crimes never even saw a courtroom. He didn't leave enough evidence.

Believe it or not, it's easier to cover up blood and bodies than it is dirty money. "Dad, he is alive and probably very sore... I just had to escape. That's why I'm here. I didn't know where else to go. I know you have ways to keep him away, so I never have to see him again."

I'm doing my best imitation of a 7-year-old me. He was my hero my whole childhood. I didn't know about all his extra activities until my mom passed. He would ride me on the lawn mower, and we'd share a bag of peanuts while sitting by the pond on the back of our land. We would watch the ducks, and he would play the harmonica and smoke a menthol. It was a perfect childhood. Now he is standing in front of me, hunched over from old age and a bad back. He's giving me that stink eye he gives people on the fence about buying an RV.

"Are you done this time? If I take you in and teach you everything I know, you can't go back. This is your final chance to start new. Make sure this is what you want." He rubs his big hands over his face and turns towards the kitchen. "Have you eaten? I was going to make some fry bread if you want some?" Talk about bringing back childhood memories. I stand at the island in the kitchen, and it's like I'm sucked back to 1999.

My dad, flouring the surface and getting ready to roll out the dough, gives me a toothy smile. Smells and sounds make my memories come to life. *Have you ever smelled bread dough frying in a pan? It's fucking magical.* It's also part of my dad's Native

American heritage. He doesn't talk about it much, but his grandmother was Choctaw, and his grandpa was straight French Cajun. That helps explain how we share the dark wavy hair and his green eyes. The most significant difference is our skin tones.

Where he is like old leather, tan and wrinkled, I'm pale and pink. I guess that's the one thing I got from my mom beside her small nose. My aunt says that side of the family was mostly French and Irish. Lots of pale skin and blonde hair. I'm snapped out of my thoughts when a plate drops in front of me. Delicious fry bread covered in butter and syrup. Dad takes his heritage lightly. I think the Navy taught him to put enough sugar on something, and it'll be good. I'm shoveling it in my mouth faster than a whore getting paid by how many ounces she can swallow.

Let me tell you a determined woman can take a lot of cum if the price is right.

I polish off my meal and look up, ready for battle. I am surprised when I see Old Man about to light up a joint. *Some shit with Frank "Old Man" Underhill never changes.* He takes a big pull, looks at me, and shrugs. "Hand it over, hard ass. I'm old enough now to share. I think we both need it for the conversation we're about to have." He grins, like I said he won the lottery, while passing it over and sitting down in the stool across from me.

I take a long drag and hold it. Letting it go, I finally feel calm enough to spill everything I need to. Here goes nothin'.

Chapter Two: Holder

Damn it! How do I always get picked for this shit? I mean yeah, I can hold my own in a fight, but so can the other fuckers.

Somehow, I get selected to babysit Old Man's daughter. She has finally come out from wherever she has been hiding. Apparently, they think she needs watching, but I still don't know why.

"They" just happen to be the heads of the most powerful families running behind the scenes in New Orleans. You could call them the mob, or the mafia, or a gang. In reality, they are just a big family that has no qualms killing, selling drugs, laundering dirty money, or anything of the illegal sort. The Saupoudrer crime syndicate is their technical moniker. Old Man did his part back in the day. He cleaned up loose ends, even did eight years for running dirty money, and never opened his mouth. He has high standing with everyone in our community.

There is no one leader in this Family. We have several heads of families that make decisions and keep the peace. Old Man never had a son, so he stepped down and went into retirement, running his RV dealership, and flying under the radar. His daughter had been a kid then. He wanted her raised like we all were, but her mother was a sweet, easy-going woman without a mean bone in her body. So, he gave in, and they raised the girl on the up and up. Until the day, his old lady never woke up. They said a brain aneurysm in her sleep. It wrecked Old Man.

Everyone showed up at the funeral and paid their respects. I was 22 at the time and didn't pay much attention. I just remembered Old Man hunched over in the pew with his hands covering his face. That was six years ago, and no one had heard much from Old Man or his daughter. Rumor is that she ran off with an older guy after her mom passed, and never came back. Until now.

Old Man finally called in a favor. I still wasn't excited to be the one stuck watching a spoiled brat. She had to be. Anyone that would run away from everything Old Man gave her, and not even look back, was as spoiled as they come. I don't have a choice, though.

Do what you're told is rule one in this Family. Don't ask questions is rule two. Rule three is the easiest. Clean up all the blood and evidence. Anything else is pretty much open to interpretation. So here I sit in my car, trying to stay cool in this summer weather, and await the princess. I'm supposed to take the brat to the RV dealership and make sure she is okay while she learns all about cleaning money. Not how I wanted to spend my day.

I'm only waiting six minutes before the door to the house opens and a woman catches my attention. That can't be the spoiled daughter everyone has been talking about. Spoiled girls don't dress like that. Long curvy legs and a thick ass covered in dark gray ripped skinny jeans. A t-shirt that looks a bit small and seen better days hides her full tits. On better inspection, I can tell her top is a concert t-shirt, for the heavy metal band Anthrax. Some old ass Chuck Taylor high tops and huge, red, round sunglasses finish off her outfit. The thing that draws my attention the most is her hair.

Everyone was talking about how the girl looked just like the Old Man. This girl was anything but. Her hair hung to her waist in loose waves and in the most shocking, but beautiful, blue color.

She was making her way down the steps of the old house when I noticed she was munching away on something. Something messy.

Oh, dear God, there she goes! Falling into a split, one foot sliding down the stairs before the other can catch up. She makes a pained face while turning on to her side. I jump out of the car and rush to her, fairly sure she just slit her twat and asshole into one giant gash.

I hear her little gasped swears, so I know she is conscious. "Mother fuckin' butt licker, son of a gottdamn donkey and monkey butt fuck!" Well, that was colorful.

"You okay there, Princess?" That earns me, what I'm guessing is, a dirty look. It's hard to tell with the huge sunglasses and hair over her face.

That's when I notice the creamy substance smeared on her face, hands, and the toast about 10 feet from us in the grass. "What the hell are you eating? Maybe that's why you pulled that gymnastics move. You really shouldn't be eating an actual meal while walking downstairs." She rips the sunglasses off her face, and I'm in shock. Her eyes are almond-shaped and soulful. A beautiful green with yellow speckled around her pupils. Even with all the beauty, she sure does look as mad as a honey badger right now. She inherited her dad's glare. The one that makes your blood run cold. The one that lets you know she has a lot of crazy behind the calm eyes.

"Excuse the fuck out of me! I got told to hurry up and get out here. That 'Holder' was waiting to take me to work. I didn't realize 'Holder' was going to be some cocky cunt muffin. I would have sat down and enjoyed my shit on a shingle in peace. Now it's ruined. Guess we know who is stopping for donuts on the way." That "I dare you to defy me" look remaining. "Besides, even if I did slip, it was classy and graceful as shit." I hear her grumble under her breath.

For fuck's sake, the mouth on that girl could make a grown man blush. She is more like her dad than I first thought, "What the hell were you eating? It doesn't sound like something to get upset over.

I'm sure you'll be okay till lunch. We're on a schedule and don't have time for stops. Let's get going before we piss off daddy." I gave her a tight-lipped smile. That might have been a little excessive seeing as it earned me another death glare.

"Look here, douchebag. I've spent too many years listening to assholes. I'm not about to listen to you. You're my damn chauffeur and nothing more."

Damn, she is feisty. "Okay. Whatever you say, Princess. You can be the one to take it up with Old Man." I'm not about to get my day started in an argument with this brat. She's gonna drive me to hit the hard stuff and I haven't even had my coffee yet. Turning my back on the new mafia princess, I head back to my still idling car, not waiting to see if she follows.

Sliding in, I turn the radio to whatever loud, sound drowning song I can find. I peer out the windshield and watch as she cusses up a storm while brushing off the remaining food and dirt. Thank goodness we don't have a bunch of Bible-thumpers around here or she'd be having a come to Jesus meeting with them ASAP. Finally, she starts her stomping trek to the car. Swinging open the door so hard, I'm surprised the hinges don't squeak in protest. "Easy on the ride! It didn't cause you to drop it low on the stairs." I'm on the receiving end of a glare so hot I'm almost sweating, but she doesn't need to know that. Play it cool Hold.

"Drive the damn car before I throat punch you

and drive it myself." I know when to just be quiet. I did grow up with a bitch of a mother and know sometimes quiet is best. I back out of the driveway and start the 20-minute drive to our destination.

"So... Where ya been hiding the last few years? Somewhere tropical and fun? Burning up Daddy's cash with the boyfriend?" I swear I see my life flash before my eyes when she grabs the wheel and snatches it. Stopping us in the open grass on the side of the road.

"Let's get everything straight right now. You are here to drive me and make sure I get where I'm going safely. Don't ask questions, don't assume anything, don't even think about me. Just keep your mouth shut and drive the fucking car."

Damn crazy bitch. I don't even glance in her direction as I take off back down the road before she changes her mind and does some other stupid shit. I stop by the donut shop, since I don't really want another battle with the hellion before getting to the lot. The quicker I can get her to work and away from me, the better my day will be.

Old Man, sitting out front smoking menthol cigarettes, watches us pull in. He is looking his age. Wonder if she came back because she knows he won't be around much longer. He stands and greets his daughter at the front door. His starched pants are so sharp you could get a cut if you got too close.

"Schatzi! How did Holder treat ya?" Old Man's years in Germany with the Navy still show through occasionally. That's one nickname I remember him using years back.

"Oh, just peachy! Ya know acted like a real fucking gentleman." She smiles a little too sweetly while digging Old Man a bear claw out of the donut box.

"Aww, Schatzi, you remembered my favorite! You ready to get to work?" Old Man dabs out his cigarette and goes at the bear claw, like a starved man.

"Whatever Old Man. Let's just get this over with so I can get back. I got other stuff to do." Big ass brat! Sitting in Cole's office, I close my eyes. I need some "me-time" if I have to drive back with her.

I hear Cole come in and quietly shut the door.

"She's already getting under your skin?" Rolling my eyes back to look up at him.

"She hasn't called you a 'cunt muffin' yet... Just wait. Here soon you'll be ready to put a pillow over her head until the noise stops." The hot cup of coffee he pushes my way is just how I like it, two sugars and a cream. Cole, me, and the other Sons of Fortune have grown up together. We might as well be real brothers; we are the oldest sons of the Saupoudrer crime syndicate. We have to have a strong bond when it comes time for us to step up to lead.

"Hold, we don't know her story. Just give her the benefit of the doubt. She might have had her reasons to run. She is easy on the eyes. So that's a plus." I can't help but shake my head. "Leave it to you to get pulled in by a pretty face. Okay, I'll cut her some slack. Just watch and see if she cuts us any slack. I'm fairly sure she hates men in general." I can't help but wonder why that is. I'm also wondering where her boyfriend is. I'm sure he'll show himself sooner or later.

"Let's make a good impression. Never know, she might stay and take Old Man's seat at the table." Cole, always the optimist. That's laughable. She isn't cut out for the life that would come with that position. "We'll worry about today first, okay? She might not even make it a week." It would be nice to have a woman at the table, but I don't see that happening.

Chapter Three: Ayida

. Fuck my life! Hot guys are buzzing around like flies, and I swore to keep my legs together till I got my shit straightened out. Dad is talking, but it's so hard to concentrate when the blond Olympian is sitting in the office across from us. I can see through the window he is leaned back in the seat with his feet kicked up on a desk, eyes closed, but still talking to the tattooed bear of a man. How is that much big dick energy in the same room together? It's like the universe's personal "fuck you" right in my face. I remember the blondes name... Holder.

Doesn't matter, I will just call him "sex-on-a-stick". Blond shaggy hair. Tallish, built like a runner. You can see long muscles under his tight jeans. Defined muscles, coming from under his shirt sleeves. A definite asshole but nothing I can't handle. He doesn't smile much. His honey colored eyes tell a lot though.

I let my eyes wander next to the beast. I have no clue who he is, but I'll call him "Sir"! Like in- "Yes Sir, you can bend me over the desk." Gottdamn this man is huge. He is easily 2 to 3 inches taller than Holder. His dark thick hair is cut short on the sides and long on top. Plenty left to hold his head down between my legs. He has tattoos covering both arms, and I can't help but wonder if he has anymore. He is all broad shoulders and thick thighs. Not body builder defined, more like he has seen a lot of hard work. He has a nice beard- dark and thick. I can imagine my cum dripping from it when I'm finally done riding his face.

I completely missed what dad was saying. I guess I need to pay more attention. "Schatzi? Did you hear anything, or are you too busy dick dreaming?"

Damn his scary good observation skills. "Yep, sure. Heard it all... So, what we gonna do now?"

He sighs and levels a, "I know your bullshit,"

look my way. "Well, if you wouldn't have been stuck staring at the boys, you would have heard me say, you'll be shadowing Cole. He is the only one that 'works' here. The other Sons have different business ventures they are in on." Hmmm, so Sir's name is Cole. I can see that. He looks like a Cole. "Go ahead and head over to his office. He'll get you started on the computer." Fine by me. More time with the man-candy.

Knocking on the door I hear a muffled, "Come in." Two sets of eyes settle on me. It's a little unnerving. I considered myself a wee bit of a badass, but I also talk a big game as far as sex goes. I've been with a few guys, but my last relationship was anything but fun times. I've had dreams of being with more than one guy, but that fantasy was never gonna happen.

Now, I feel like my future might just be changing right before my eyes. "Hey, I'm Cole! You must be Ayida. How's it going?" Damn, his voice is like whiskey. Shocking in the heat, but a smooth finish that makes you come back for more. He is giving me this disarming smile and it's fucking beautiful. He is what I imagine the definition of a real man is. All smoky sex appeal wrapped in tattoos and tan skin. I have a feeling, "Yes sir," is going to be a big part of my vocabulary very soon.

"I'm fine. Need some coffee...all the coffee. Death before decaf!" I might be drooling, watching the cup moving to Holder's mouth.

"That I can do! You want cream or French

vanilla?"

"Black, please. I need the hot blackness to restore my graying soul." He looks at me skeptically but shrugs and leaves to get me a cup...or 3.

I can feel Holder's eyes on me. "I didn't realize you had tats and everything." He does a very vague hand wave to my face. Why do people always do that? Gesture to your whole person, like it's offensive. That's another reason I didn't fit in the little Tennessee town I ran from. There, little old ladies at the Lucky's Grocery would always turn their lips up sneering, look at me up and down and just shake their heads. Fucking Jurassic bitches.

"Yep. You were probably too busy judging everything else about me." He is still studying my arms, neck, and face.

"I was busy watching you do a stripper move on the front steps. Also, your creative cursing was a little distracting, as well as your charming personality. I do like the ink though. Does any of it mean anything?"

I'm a little shocked he seems interested. Most guys don't like all the colorful images running down my arms and up my neck. "I mean, they all mean something to me. I have one in memory of my mom here." I point to the fairy holding a rose on my forearm. "I have some of my favorite things, things that remind me of the good and bad times. I have some covering my scars. Either way, I love them all." I take the time to admire my comic book symbols, hearts, flowers, food, characters, and just a plethora of colors. The story of my long 24 years.

"They are beautiful. I don't have any myself, but you probably saw Cole has enough for both of us. What about the face jewelry? Is it all real?"

"Do you really think I got all this ink just to puss out on the piercings?" I pull on my Medusa, above my lip, and stick my tongue out. "I have other ones also." Rubbing the bar around my lips, displaying my tongue ring, and giving him the side-eye.

"I bet you do. You don't seem like the kind of girl that does stuff half ass." He is smiling this time. Damn, it's pretty like the rest of him.

The door opens with a creak; Cole is pushing it with his firm round ass. Damn, I just want a little touch, lick, bite... Anything! Get a hold of yourself! You are a strong independent woman! You don't need a firm, tight tush. Ahhh, stop being a slut, brain. Cole is staring at me like I had a stroke. To his credit, I probably look like I did. Ya know inner monologue going wild.

"Everything copacetic in here?" His eyes darting between Holder and me.

"Yep, just talking ink and needles. Princess here has more piercings than what you can see with clothes on." He just has to ruin our vibe with his sexist nickname. I look over at Cole, he is looking at my tits like he can see through my shirt; maybe he can, mine are pierced after all. Nipples are always a mind fuck.

"If you're going to start nicknames, I would much prefer bitch, slut, cunt, heifer... really anything other than princess or other girly names."

He is smiling again, but this is a shit-eating grin. "Heifer? Care to explain?" I roll my eyes.

"You know, stubborn, hard-headed, chunky girl. Will run you over if provoked or for food."

Cole is actually laughing now. Holder is just looking at his lap, shaking his head, but I do see a small upturn of his lips. "Thick is what I would call you. Curvy... Luscious, but yeah, hard-headed fits too." I'm in complete shock, and that doesn't happen often.

Holder is grinning, but not at me. His gaze is on Cole. Cole's eyes are on my jean-clad legs. Roaming up and down, examining the rips and tears. Finally, he passes me my huge thermos of piping hot coffee. "Mmmm!" I may have just moaned out loud as I feel the heat in my hands, and that first sip bringing new life to my body. It's almost like shaking the dust from my spirit. Yep, definitely moaned as I notice Holder staring at my lips, and Cole adjusting a not so inconspicuous bulge in his pants. Seriously, is that dude huge everywhere?

Clearing his throat, Cole refocuses, "So let's get down to business. I'm guessing you have basic computer skills?"

Two hours later, I'm stiff and ready to get up and move around. I already knew about title work from helping Old Man when I was a teenager over the summers. I have a good idea about the financial systems too. Cole showed me how to keep up with inventory, what was out for repairs, what was a trade-in, and what all his notes meant.

The biggest thing about laundering money is that the cover business has to be authentic. Luckily, it is, and that was what we mostly went through. I think Old Man just wants to keep me as an office clerk and not show me the real dark side of everything. But that's no longer my reality if I want my new life to work. He is still trying to shelter me like Momma wanted. Problem with that was, I had been so sheltered I didn't know the devil until he was standing over me with hate in his eyes and his hands in fists. It could have gone two ways. One, I could have stayed down and maybe ended up dead, or two let the real evil take a piece of me and my humanity. So, when I finally beat my ex bloody, I laughed about it and felt pure pleasure while the droplets hit my face, thus confirming I chose the latter way.

Dad did what he thought was best for me growing up but sheltering me can only go so far when I'm destined for the dark side in this Family. It's time to put up or shut up. Besides, now I like the black, dirty, shadows, and plan on staying there. Time to make friends with my inner monsters and have some fun.

Standing up from the office chair and stretching. I've finished three thermoses of coffee and have to pee NOW. Pushing past the guys beside me, I head to the restroom.

After washing my hands, I push through the door just to run face first into a hard chest. "What the fuck? My nose..." I trail off as my eyes take in the bright green set opposite from me. Green pastures after a spring rain. I just want to roll around in... with him. I back up and take in the rest of him. His smile is broad and framed by full lips. Hair the color of blood after it's started to dry. A deep rusty red, spiked up on top. He isn't overly tall. My nose is at his sternum. I could just lean up and lick the sensitive skin at the base of his throat. No! Stop it! Control your vajayjay! I step back a bit more. He is still smiling at me and it is fucking adorable. I swear to God I am smitten at first glance. This dude is certifiably lickable. Deep breaths Ayida, deep breaths.

"Hi! I'm Fletcher, but you, precious, can call me Fletch." He steps forward into my personal space beaming at me.

"I'm Ayida, Ayida Underhill. Sorry about breaking my nose on you." Why didn't I correct the nickname? Because he is damn squeezable and has dimples. Those damn gorgeous dimples could easily be the death of me, so he gets a pass this time. I mean, I did try to tackle him.

"Oh, your Old Man's girl. What is it he calls you?" He looks me over like he is looking for a clue. You can see when it clicks. "Schatzi! It means sweetheart, right?"

Here we go… "Yeah, we had an agreement he

could call me a girl name if it were in a different language, so it didn't sound so girly."

He takes another step closer, pushing me back towards the door. "I like that. Are you really sweet, though? I mean, I bet you taste sweet, but you look like you carry some attitude around." He licks his lips, and I squeeze my thighs together.

Damn it. It's been a long time since I had someone make me wet, with or without touching. I'm fucking soaked now. This man doesn't know what he's starting. *I will screw him six ways from Sunday.* I made a promise to get my shit together and finish business before getting involved with anyone, but getting orgasms doesn't mean being involved, does it? I could do "no strings attached" after the history I've had. I shake my head and smile sweetly at him. I move my hand up his chest and quickly slide to the side, away from him and his panty soaking eyes, mouth, dimples, body. Damn. I walk back to the office without looking back

Chapter Four: Fletcher

Struck. I don't know how else to put it. Her hair reminds me of lightning, and that's precisely what she has done—struck me with a force that has me standing in the hallway, with a still hardening dick, watching her walk away. Her ass is round and thick. I imagine it would bounce really good while she was bent over, with me pounding into her. I would totally eat her pussy from the back just so I could see her ass jiggle when she came on my face.

Okay, I have to stop before I end up with a wet spot on my pants. I adjust myself and head in the direction she went. Not because I'm looking for her. I'm looking for my brother. I mean, I wouldn't be upset if she ran into me again. Holder is supposed to be here. I don't know why, but that's what his sister said when I went by his house. She had started living with him when she dropped out of school, and their parents were giving her a hard time. That's Holder for you, though. He loves his sister.

I see the shaggy blond hair through the window of Cole's office. I should have known he would be here hanging out, helping Cole. What I didn't expect was the wild-looking Ayida sitting between them when I walked in.

She's trying to talk her way out of more work. Girl after my own heart. "Please! I've done what you said. Can I please just get lunch? I have other stuff I'm working on." She is so beautiful and using her looks to get her way with the guys. Bottom lip stuck out, and her head tilted down so her eyes look more prominent and innocent. She is a wolf in sheep's clothing, and she is going to be the end of us. Looks like fun, though.

"What the hell you got to do?" Holder questions, being charming, as always. He could be charming if he wants, but we're still the monsters in this city. The monsters that kept the others in line.

That's why I was looking for him now, to let him know about our last job.

"Well, we got the thumbs up from our last client. Why don't we make it an early day and go celebrate?"

She's looking at me like I had just handed her a puppy. She might have a body full of tattoos and piercings, but her face still looks like an innocent girl that needs my help.

"Thank you! See, Fletch agrees. I'm ready to eat, y'all can drop me off at Old Man's, and I can do what I need to do." I think I just made a friend. "Well, you all heard the lady. Let's get out of here before her pop catches us sneaking her out." They look at each other and shrug. I have won the battle!

Piling in my SUV we head towards Commerce Street. I don't even ask for opinions, I'm going to my favorite place, and everyone can kiss my ass. Judy's Place is a little hole-in-the-wall that serves Cajun, French, American, and a bunch of crap I think Judy just made up. Noticing their weird looks, I realize a crooning love song is softly playing in the background. I'm not exactly the hardcore kind of guy like the other Sons. Don't get me wrong I'll get my hands dirty, but I like the classics and have a love of art and literature. I know this isn't their idea of good music, so I switch my playlists to something more "badass." The guys seem happy and more at ease now that the love song is over.

Bunch of pussies can't deal with emotions or anything beyond blood and pain. They call me the runt of the group, but at least I'm not scared of showing other sides of myself than just the violent son of an asshole. I notice Ayida looks a little more relaxed too. I guess she isn't comfortable with feelings either, or she just has shit taste in music. I clear my throat and cut my eyes to the blue-haired beauty sitting next to me. *I'm a gentleman and made sure she got the shotgun seat.* "So, if you don't mind me asking, why the blue hair?"

Catching her off guard, her cheeks tinge pink while she runs a hand through said hair. "Well, I've only had it blue for a few weeks. It was my natural brown. When I moved here, I figured it was a new start, a new me. Might as well do something to change my appearance. Blue just seemed to fit my attitude at the time. Not depressed but dealing with some shit." Hmmm, well seems we got some deeper stuff going on here than just a daddy's girl coming home for the money.

"While we're on a personal subject, why did you come home after all this time?"

Her eyes went dark, and I swear the temperature dropped in the car. "That is my business, and I'm not in the mood to talk about it." She shut that shit down real quick.

"Okay, what do you do for fun?" Never corner a wild animal, always give them an easy out, or you might get your face mauled the fuck off.

"I don't know. I haven't had a lot of fun in the last few years. I guess getting tats and piercings is my version of fun. Well that and baking." Aww, little homemaker in a killer costume.

"I wouldn't mind trying your muffin sometime." Okay, so it was cheesy, but I couldn't help it. At least it got me a little smirk.

"I don't think you can handle my muffin." Damn. I'm really gonna like this girl.

Turning into Judy's I hear a loud groan; to my surprise it is the little badass next to me and not the guys. They're too busy whispering in the back like a bunch of old women to pay any attention.

"Not you too! Old Man loves this place. We were here all the time growing up. Judy might as well be my godmother," she whimpers.

One of the reasons I love this place is because

all the Family eats here, and nothing gets by Judy. Any info you may need you can get from her.

"They have the best étouffée in the whole city. Humor me and eat here and I'll get you some beignets for dessert." Girls like sweet shit, right?

"How about you buy me a beer with my lunch, and we'll call it even?" Well, okay, should have seen that coming.

"Deal! Let's eat. Oh yeah, forgot to tell y'all. Clint is meeting us here. He just got back in town last night and wanted to fill us in on what's going on up north." Ayida turns her curious gaze towards me, and all I can think is, I wish I could look at her all the time.

"Who is Clint? I don't know if Old Man wants me

to meet the whole Family in one day without him." She seems nervous, but I guess I would be too meeting another one of the Family.

"He is the other head son in the Family. Like us three, he'll take over for his family when his father passes on."

Her eyes spark up in recognition. "I didn't realize y'all was 'The Sons of Fortune'. I thought Holder here was a lackey of Old Man's. It makes a lot more sense now. He is a privileged prick." Her taunts are getting the effect she wanted. Holder is red across the nose, giving a pretty stern glare in her direction, and crossing his arms tightly.

"Now listen here, you spoiled brat. You don't get to come in here and make assumptions about us. You're the one that ran away with the first man that gave you attention instead of staying and helping Old Man and taking a seat at the table when his time comes. Now he had to let his family name go because you were too busy with your new life, with your boyfriend. Keep your assessments to yourself."

Oh yeah, she pissed off Hold, but apparently, he had pushed the right buttons because she's striding up to him with death in her eyes, and her fists balled up at her sides. Before anyone could blink, she sucker-punched him right in the nose, sending a spray of blood over his shirt and her shoes. I run to pull her back. I'm not worried about Hold hurting her, but I am worried she might hit him again now that his hands are covering his eyes.

"What the fuck? You bitch!"

She is still seething. "Don't fucking talk about my dad or my life like you know anything. I was just joking about the prick comment, but I guess it was on the nose, huh?" Damn, this girl is savage. Hold gets the bleeding under control and is cleaning up, growling and grumbling. I need to calm this situation fast.

"Okay, Baby Girl, I know he pissed you off after you pissed him off, but no need in hitting. Let's eat and see if we can go back to being civil. Can we at least try? Everyone will be on their best behavior. Pinky promise." She gives me a shy smile, the complete opposite of the wild animal that was going for blood a minute ago.

"Okay. I'll do my best not to rip his eyes out as long as he stays far away from me." Cole, who has been standing beside Hold in complete shock this entire time, decides to break down cackling.

"Damn, girl! You are crazy like Old Man." He's not lying. This girl would fit in just fine with our little group of couillons.

Chapter Five: Clint

Hot damn! Judy knows how to make a mean burger. I'm just sitting there, minding my own business when the door slings open, the air went out, and my breath catches in my chest. She is my teenage dream come to life, and everything my mom would hate. Blue hair, piercings, and tattoos everywhere. I thought for sure my taste had changed over the last ten years, but the tightness in my pants tells me I've been very wrong.

I'm even more surprised when my best friends *basically brothers* file in behind her like the teacher had reprimanded them. Now that they are getting closer, I can tell Hold looks like a UFC fighter knocked him the fuck out.

"What the hell happened? Did y'all go on a job without telling anyone?"

"Little Miss Attitude" is giving me a strange almost ravenous look. Kind of how I looked at my hamburger when the waitress brought it out. "Hold doesn't know how to bite his tongue and figured out pretty quick Baby Girl here has a mean right hook." Cole looks damn happy about the whole situation.

Hold looks ready to commit murder. Poor Fletcher caught in between. I know right away I'm going to like this girl.

It's easy to figure out who she is. These guys don't take girls to lunch, or anywhere for that matter. So, this has to be Old Man's daughter. She has her pop's mean look. Its laser aimed at Hold now. They are just staring at each other like two dogs about to lock up in a fight. Whatever he did must have been pretty bad.

"So, you must be Ayida. How's it being back home?" She looks a little shocked but gives me a small smile.

"It was going pretty good till him." She throws her thumb over her shoulder toward Hold.

"Oh, he is always surly this time of the year. It's the heat. Poor guy can't handle the humidity." That pulls a laugh from everyone but said person.

"You must be Clint. I think we'll get along fine. Now Fletch, what were you saying about a beer?" Fletcher smirks while throwing an arm over her shoulders and leads her to the front to order. Cole and Holder take their seats; Holder sitting way back, legs crossed, with his hands folded in his lap, and looking very closed off from any potential conversation.

"So, what the fuck did you do, man? Don't you know better than to piss Old Man's daughter off on the first day?" He looks up from his lap to give me a scathing glare.

"She has been getting on my nerves all day. Well, there were those few minutes in the office where I thought I could like her, but that didn't last long."

All I can do is shake my head. Holder won't ever open up to anyone. Dude seriously thinks having any kind of feelings, or getting serious with a girl, makes him weak- a liability. It has to be from his fucked-up mom and dad. I mean, my family is fucked up too, but in a whole different way. My mom just wants me to settle down with a calm, easily managed girl. Fitting in with the rest of the Family. Dad doesn't care as long as Mom is happy. He really does love her and has set a good example of how to love a woman even when she is bat shit crazy. Mom was one of the many reasons I enlisted in the Navy. Old

Man was another. He gave me the push I needed. I got away and became my own man.

Hold's mom and dad, both of them, are fucked in the head. They couldn't stand each other and didn't do anything to hide it. They cheated every chance they could. His mom stayed gone most of the time, and his dad wasn't much better. Hold was usually at one of our houses growing up; he did the best he could with what he had.

We sit in silence until Fletcher shows back up with Ayida carrying trays of food. After everyone starts digging in, I start my questioning. "So, Ayida, that's an interesting name... What's it means?" She swallows a fried oyster and nods her head.

"I don't know a ton about it, but she is a Loa, a

goddess or spirit in Louisiana and Haitian Vodou. The rainbow and snake represent her. She also has a lot to do with fertility in the culture." She takes a breath before finishing like she has to work up the nerve to say what she has to say. "My mom had several miscarriages before me. She didn't think she would ever have kids. She was religious, but desperate. She saw a Vodou lady before she got pregnant with me. The lady gave my mom some stuff to drink and boom I was there nine months later. So, my mom named me after the goddess the lady said gave me to her."

I didn't see that coming. "That's awesome. I just got named after my dad's favorite actor. I bet you can guess who that is." She's giggling now.

"I have a rather good idea. I like Clint, though. It's unique." She resumes her meal, making little slurping sounds as she drinks her beer. From the looks of the other guys, well all of us besides Hold, we all like her sounds.

"How is living back with Old Man? Is he as scary as he seems, or is he a big softy?"

She doesn't even look up from her food to answer. "He is my dad, so of course he isn't scary to me. Now, y'all he would gut before you could blink. He might be old, but he is mean as they come. If he doesn't like you, you might as well move out of Louisiana. He is gonna make your life miserable." I guess I'm one lucky fucker. Old Man likes that I'm ex-Navy like him.

"Good to know. What about you? Are you as mean as you look?" Smirking, she cuts her eyes over to me.

"Oh, I'm much worse than I look." Message received loud and clear. Don't fuck with the rainbow.

"Is everyone done, chit-chatting? Let's get Princess here back home. We have business to discuss." That guy is just burying himself deeper and deeper. She just rolls her eyes and pushes up from the table. I guess Q and A is over then. I didn't even get to the good stuff yet. Damn you, Holder.

Chapter Six: Ayida

"This heat is gonna kill me." I like my air conditioning. Just walking out of Judy's into the humid Louisiana summer heat is pure, fucking torture. I'm sweating like a whore in church. At least I did get my belly full and learned a little about the guys I'm now surrounded by. Three of the four hotties seem like guys I could definitely enjoy spending lots of time with. Hold can kiss my sweet white ass.

I don't know what made him dislike me so much, or presume I am a bitch, but I'm about to handle the situation. I didn't leave the hell hole I was in to get talked down to, and I certainly won't lower my standards for anyone like Holder.

"If y'all don't mind dropping me off at home, I have some stuff to take care of." I need to do some recon and make sure my ex is staying his ass in Tennessee and the hell away from me. I know Old Man will keep me safe, but I would rather not bring the fight to his front door. If it comes down to it, I'll take care of him before he causes problems. Having access to weapons, and unlimited swamp land to hide bodies, makes me feel a little more empowered.

"You still with us, Blue?" I blink back to reality. Clint, leaning against the SUV, is smiling at me with laughter in his gorgeous stormy blue eyes. He is shorter than Cole, but still around 6'2". His caramel-colored hair is short and combed to the side. He has an old school style. He looks muscled up, and you can tell he takes pride in staying in shape. His handsome face is covered in a dusting of hair. I want to feel the stubble on my thighs.

"Sorry. Just have a lot on my mind. Interesting nickname, I like it better than Princess." His smile is gorgeous. How am I gonna stay focused with these guys hanging around?

"Well, it fits with that hair. I don't know if I've ever seen someone look so good with blue hair. It fits you." Okay, I can't help but blush.

That was one of the best compliments I've ever received. I mean, I haven't had many compliments in my life. It's not hard to impress me. "Thank you. I was a mousey brown a few weeks ago when I first moved back. I decided I needed more of a change. Blue reminds me of the water. Water is always moving, but it's also strong enough to change stone. I felt like that fit me. I wanted change, but also strength. I want to sculpt my future to what I want."

Damn, I went a little too deep. I can feel all their eyes on me. "Sorry. Got a little in my head." I start to get in the car and feel a hand on my shoulder. I don't know what happened next, but when I open my eyes, I'm on the pavement next to the SUV. Clint is holding his hand, cussing up a storm. Holder and Cole are standing between him and me. Fletcher is kneeling next to me, but careful to keep his hands to himself.

"You back with us?" He seems unsure of what to say or if he is even talking to a person.

I look down and notice my arms tight around my knees, and I feel myself slightly rocking back and forth. "What happened? How did I get down here? Is Clint okay?" I'm starting to really panic. "Clint was going to offer you a ride home, but when he touched you, I don't know how to explain it, but you grabbed his fingers and bent them backward. You dropped to the ground and started mumbling. Clint is okay. I think you just sprained or dislocated his fingers. Are you okay? Do we need to call Old Man?"

Oh shit. Even after getting away, that asshole is still fucking my life up. "No! I'm okay. I'm so sorry, Clint!" Aww damn, here comes the tears. I said no more crying a long time ago. I learned quickly that crying made everything worse. Robert would scream and hit harder, yelling at me to shut my damn mouth. I have never intentionally hurt an innocent person before, and my emotions are taking on a life of their own. Clint is just staring at me. He probably thinks I'm crazy. I'll probably never see him again, and that's for the best. I'm too fucked up for friends.

"Baby Blue, who the fuck hurt you so bad? I want to know. They will never hurt you again." I'm shocked. This is the first time in years I've done something wrong and am still able to walk away after it. More than that, he wants to protect me. He isn't even yelling at me.

"I'm sorry. I didn't mean to. I just want to go home." He inches forward towards me with his hands out.

"Can I help you up, please?" I look at his hands. They are rough and calloused. His eyes are pleading, and I don't want to hurt him anymore. Reaching out, I grab his hand, and he hauls me up. I'm standing inches from him, and he smells like cinnamon and leather. Looking in his eyes, I see understanding, but

I don't know how that's possible. "Don't apologize, Baby Blue. I know what PTSD looks like, and you didn't mean to hurt me. That was your fight or flight kicking in."

I don't even know what to say. So, I just reach around him and squeeze. My face presses against his chest and tears stream down my face. I feel my body relax. Tension leaking from my muscles. I didn't know I was so tight. I hardly know this man. I've only been talking to him for an hour, but the way he looked at me. The way he spoke to me. He didn't even get mad when I hurt him. He is the polar opposite of Robert.

He wraps his arms around my shoulders, and I let go of a breath I didn't know I was holding. It's just pure warm comfort. Is this what human contact is supposed to feel like? Is this what I've been missing? I pull away to look at his face. He smiles down at me, and I feel it in my gut. He is a good man. I know that because I've seen evil men and this man is far from that. "I'm so sorry. Are you okay?" He just chuckles. I can feel the vibration, and then I remember, I'm hanging on to him like an opossum on a limb. Jerking back with a blush, I mumble another apology. Old habits die hard.

"Stop with the apologies. You left a sore spot, but I'm fine! I'm ex-Navy like Old Man. You will have to do a lot worse than that to scare me off." He wiggles his fingers in front of me to show he still has use of the digits. "Now, would you like a ride home from me? The other guys really need to get back to work."

Looking around, I remember we are not alone. Cole and Fletcher are watching me like I'm a sideshow freak. Holder is giving me the same old stink eye. I think I like his reaction better than the others. I've had enough weird or pitying looks during my life. "You sure you don't mind?" He grabs my hand and starts leading me to a car a few spots away. "See you guys later. Thanks for the beer, Fletcher!" That's the only goodbye I have a chance to give before Clint is opening the door to a seventy model Chevelle. It's black with white stripes running down the middle. It's gorgeous. "Damn, this is a dream car! How long have you had her?" Sliding across the warm leather seat. He shuts my door and makes his way to the driver's side.

"I got the body right when I got home from my first tour. I didn't get started working on her until I got discharged after being hurt. She has looked like this for about two years." He reaches into the console and pulls out some cinnamon gum. His smell is starting to make more sense.

"Well, you did a fantastic job..." I'm fumbling for small talk. I've never been big on it anyway. I was "encouraged" to stay silent for the most part with Robert. I'm still relearning normal human interaction. I feel the deep rumble of the engine when he cranks his baby up. It feels damn good. Almost like a massage. He put a lot of time in this car. He must have a ton of patience.

He turns his body towards me, and even though

I'm trying to avoid eye contact, I find myself trapped in his stare. "Want to tell me about what happened? You don't have to, but if you want to... need to. *I'm here.* I'll stay quiet and just listen." How do I answer that? I've been trying to hide from the truth since the first time I got hit. Even after I got my revenge, I decided to act harsh and cold, but really, I've just been hiding from the memories. I mean, don't get me wrong... I'm not scared of him anymore, but I am afraid of being trapped in my head with my thoughts. It's easier just to pretend the last 6 years didn't happen.

Losing Momma and running from everything right into the arms of a monster. I just want to forget everything. I guess I can't live like that, though. That's how I ended up trying to rip Clint's fingers off.

Time to talk to someone. At least this is free. I tried the shrink after Mom, and all that did was make me angry at the world. Angry at myself. Being a teenager with big feelings is hard as fuck, and we do ridiculous irresponsible teenage stuff. Oh well, here we go, let's unpack some baggage on a clueless sexy guy since I'm all about doing stupid shit.

Chapter Seven: Clint

She looks so damn sad. I just want to make her feel better. *She is literally breaking my heart.* I know better than most how it feels to suffer in silence. Scared to say anything. Not wanting to be the freak with PTSD. Hoping it will just go away on its own and fucking up your life in the process, but I can't make it better for her. She has to want help. What can I say- darkness recognizes darkness...

Her shoulders hang down, she turns her head towards the window and starts drawing circles on her long legs with her fingernails. "Well, since I've never talked about this, I don't know where to start." I just want to touch her. To smell her again. She was like the air after a good rain. Fresh and new, but also like hot asphalt after the storm. Steamy and warm. She is a walking contradiction. Hard on the outside but torn apart and hurt on the inside.

I didn't mean to scare her. She was standing at Fletcher's SUV, and next thing I knew, she had grabbed my fingers off her shoulder and bent them until they popped. I was mad from the pain at first. Then I looked down and saw her wrapped around herself on the ground, and my heart was in my throat. I've been there. I recognized her glazed over vacant eyes. I've seen it before in myself reflected in the mirror. Man, I feel like shit for putting her in this position.

"Start from the beginning then. Everything has a beginning." Nodding her head and pushing her shoulders back, strengthening herself for memories she doesn't want.

"Well, everyone knows the start. Mom laid down for a nap and never woke up. I was there holding her when she started gasping for breath. I only saw her eyes open one more time, when the EMT pulled them open to check. That's how I'll always remember my mom. Laying in my arms, dying. We had the funeral, and the next thing I know, I was learning what life was really like. People I never knew showing up at our house. Things were happening. I just didn't understand," she pauses and takes a few deep breaths.

"I didn't want the confusion and stress that was pushed on me. So, I did what I do best. I ran. I met a man named Robert. He was 17 years older than me and he promised me the world. I was so desperate for happiness that I believed everything he said. Never even questioned it. Pathetic, right?" She sighs heavily.

"It was okay for a little bit. He wasn't perfect, but we had a good time. Then one day, he snapped at me for leaving hair in the bathtub. I thought he was just having a bad day. Then there was the screaming for not having his breakfast ready when he woke up. I found his secret cell phone. Tons of messages from young girls like me. He promised them the same things that he did to me. Love and friendship. He went crazy when I confronted him. He pushed me into the dresser and screamed in my face. I still remember the knobs pushing into my back. When he let me go, I ran for the phone. He jerked the cord from the wall and threw it across the room. I didn't know what to do, so I just started crying and begging. It made him even angrier. He locked me in the closet for 4 hours. Only to be pulled out and kicked in the stomach and chest repeatedly. Never the face though. He didn't want any obvious visible evidence of his crimes." She starts to shrink away again.

"It just got worse. Not every day, but every few days he would go off about something. I was scared to even talk or look him in the eye. It got to the point he would leave me for over forty-eight hours with no food or drinks. I wouldn't have my car or a phone. If I tried to tell anyone, he would make me look crazy and lie about everything. He had his friends believing I was the cheater and insane. The last time I tried to reach out for help, he beat me so bad I had broken ribs and fingers. He dragged me to the closet by my hair just to lock me away for 12 hours as punishment."

I can see the ghosts of the memories playing behind her eyes now. "I soon found out he was doing hardcore drugs and drinking. Bribing women to sleep with him in trade for drugs. If he couldn't get a woman to sleep with him, he would come for me. I knew better than to fight back. I would just get the shit kicked out of me and it hurts to get fucked with a broken rib. Finally, one day he came home after being gone for days, strung out on meth. He wanted a blowjob or quick fuck. He fell on the bed, and his eyes rolled back in his head, and I lost it. I've never felt like that before. I just wanted to hurt him. I wanted him to feel just a portion of what he did to me. I needed him to suffer."

She's starting to shake a little as she continues, "I found a rod and beat him. I can still feel the wood in my hands. I know what it means to white knuckle something now. After he was bloody and covered in bruises, I grabbed the handful of clothes that I was allowed and took off in my car. That's how I ended up here a few months back. I've been dealing with stuff and getting my head together before meeting the Family. I didn't want to be known as Old Man's fucked up daughter. Little late now, though. I'm sure the guys will tell their parents."

Her head is down, her hands clasped. Little wispy breaths escape her throat, and I feel so much rage. I want to hunt the fucker down and skin him alive. No real man hits on a woman. Only cowards do fuck-boy shit like that. I want to reach for her, comfort her, but I don't want to scare her again. How could anyone look at this beautiful creature and want to snuff out the light coming from her? She is stronger than she gives herself credit for. She didn't just leave the fucktard. She left her mark on him as well. I would be willing to bet he has some scars to remind him of what he lost. More than that, she survived. It takes strength to make it out of a war alive, and that's precisely what she was in.

I clear my throat, hoping she will look at me. When those gold-flecked eyes reach mine, my throat goes dry. Moisture building up in the corners make them sparkle even more. I want nothing more than to protect and comfort her. "You are a fighter. Look how much you have overcome. Please don't give up now." I take a steadying breath, "Can I hug you? If you're not comfortable, I understand." She gives me the sweetest grin and lunges across the gear shifter to wrap her colorful arms around my waist. Her electric blue hair brushing my jaw. I feel the heavy breaths leaving her body in a shudder.

That smell of rain hits me, and I make the decision right then, I'm going to be getting awfully familiar with this little spitfire.

Chapter Eight: Holder

Fuck... That was intense. I mean, the girl annoys the shit out of me, but that was hard to watch. What happens to a person to bring them that much fear? I have seen it in grown men before. When I was standing over their bodies, but those are bad men. Killers and rapists. Even if she is a brat, she doesn't deserve that. I hope Clint is okay with her. He has gone through his own shit. Who knows maybe they will be right for each other? It's not like she would want my help. I thoroughly pissed her off with my smart-ass remarks. My face is still throbbing. That girl has bigger balls than most men I know. She might just make it in this kind of life.

The other guys are lost in thought also. I can already tell Cole and Fletcher have a thing for the Blue Demon. I hope this doesn't mess up our plans. We have been groomed to take over since we could walk. Having the new girl fuck us up now doesn't work for me. I'm tired of being under the fathers' thumbs. I'm ready to rule.

"Do y'all think Clint can handle this? It hasn't been long since he was the one on the ground crying." Cole looks like he could turn someone inside out, but he really is a good guy.

"He'll be fine. She was already calming down when they left. We have work to do anyway." Fletcher, still driving, fingers clench the steering wheel.

"We have work, but she is also our job. You already fucked it up. I just hope Clint can fix this. I don't want to be on Old Man's radar for hurting his little girl."

I've heard the stories of what that crazy old bastard likes to do to his enemies. It's not pretty. I have a feeling that, for Ayida, he would burn down the city. It's not like he has a lot left to live for. Better to keep the princess happy and stay on Old Man's good side. I guess I'll be learning to hold my tongue better. I still wouldn't mind using it on her, though. Even if she is bat shit crazy, she is hot as hell. I feel all the blood rush to my dick, just thinking about her beautiful angry face.

"What ya thinking about there, Hold?" Fletch's mischievous eyes are on my crotch. Damn it. Caught tented in the front seat.

"Just an after-effect hard-on from getting hit. You know I like it rough." He laughs, but I can tell he doesn't believe that. Everyone knows I love my kink, but it would take more than a little slap to get me going. I don't mind being in control, but sometimes it's nice to let the reins go and let someone else be in charge.

"Sure, man. I get it. She is gorgeous. I doubt Old Man wants her to get messed up with us even if she is learning the business. He probably wants her with a nice guy that can be easily managed. You can look at her and tell she has had one too many assholes telling her what to do." He isn't wrong; she has been through some shit. That's obvious, but I think Clint or Cole, hell, even Fletcher would be good for her. Not me, though. I'm too rough around the edges, and even if I like to be submissive in the bedroom, in real life, I have to be in control. It's the only way to make sure everything gets done, and everyone stays alive. She's had enough trauma in her life without me messing her up even more. She sure is beautiful, though.

"Dude, we all know you like her. You have to

stop sabotaging yourself. You don't have to be a jerkoff to everyone. You can have friends and more. She needs friends, and you are a good one to have when your head isn't stuck up your ass." I can feel Cole's hard stare from the backseat. He doesn't understand how hard it is. He is friendly, and people automatically feel at ease with him. He smiles, and women fall over themselves to be near him. I can't blame them. He has that sweet, but "bad boy" look. I know what really happens. I let myself get close to someone, they find out what I've done... what I do... they see the darkness in me and run like the devil himself is chasing them.

After the years of chasing relationships, I'm finally okay with one-night stands and meaningless meetups. My brothers are the only people I need in my life. They talk a big game, but they haven't had real relationships in years either. The difference between them and me, I like what I do, and then I feel bad about wanting it. Why am I so fucked in the head? Did my fucked-up parents mess me up, too? I've never told anyone how I feel about what I do. The guys have different feelings about the jobs we do. They never volunteer for the dirty work. They don't mind the white-collar crime. Hell, they like kicking the shit out of any woman-beater that is brought to the Family's attention, but that is about their limit to violence. My shadows run darker.

Maybe one day I'll find another fucked up soul. For now, I'm good at keeping my distance and having my fun.

"All in your head again, huh? Let's just get done with today and see what we can get into tonight. "Fletcher will always be a college boy at heart. It's one of the reasons we simultaneously love and loathe him.

"Are we talking about a party or club? Do you think Clint would want to come after today? He might just want to chill at his place." Cole might have the bad boy look, but he really is just a nerd that likes to stay home and play on his Xbox or master a new hobby. The man is a kick-ass cook after his year-long obsession with all things Bobby Flay. I think he's trying out sculpting now. He succeeds in everything he does. I'm not jealous, I'm proud.

I feel like we push each other, and that makes

us better in different ways. We work best as a group. Cole is our nerdy-nice guy, Fletcher is the fun-outgoing guy, Clint is the big brother with an even bigger heart. Then there's me. The fucked-up sadist and masochist rolled up in one. I'm the lucky one. I have these guys to keep me from spiraling. They help balance me out.

"Let's see if he wants to have a little get together at his place so we can all unwind." Fletcher says, grinning like a Cheshire Cat.

Let the party begin.

Chapter Nine: Cole

Why the fuck do we have to do anything tonight? Clint probably just wants to be left alone and get his head straight. Sitting at my desk moving numbers around on the screen of my computer, I'm bored as hell and want to go play the new Call of Duty. Holder, sitting across from me with his feet thrown up and eyes closed, is getting on my last damn nerve. How can he be so cool after everything that happened today? That poor girl is messed up and he acted like it was no big deal. "You think Ayida is okay? I hope Clint got her home." I get a grunt in response. I swear to God I'm going to flip his feet over his fucking head...

"Hey. Douchebag. Remember our talk in the car? Pull your head out of your ass. She has been hurt. I know we are used to hurting bad guys, but have you become so numb that it didn't bother you when that girl was so scared, she turned into a feral animal?" He swings his legs down, straightens up with a stretch and a yawn.

"It's none of my business and you need to stay out of it too. I'm not about to get our positions messed up by a pair of long legs. She is just another girl. She'll run away again before long." He gives me a hard look before getting up and leaving my office. I want to throw my keyboard at his retreating head. I don't know what has happened to my friend, my brother, but he wasn't always like this. He used to care.

Ugh... I'll worry about him later. I have other things to concentrate on. I have to get done with these spreadsheets and try to convince Fletcher it's not a good idea to go to Clint's. I would like to go check on Ayida though. I might run by Old Man's after work and make sure we didn't do any lasting damage. I know she saw my shock when she came back from her black out. I don't want her to think we don't like her just because she has demons. We all carry those around. At least I have my friends to help carry mine. She probably doesn't have anyone. I'm sure Clint is making her feel welcome, but I want to help her, too.

I haven't been through anything like Clint has, but I do have my share of trauma. I use flirting as a coping mechanism. I always have girls trying to get me to settle down. So, I flirt a little and then get the hell out of dodge. That way I don't hurt anyone's feelings because I'm not committed. I haven't met the right girl to chill with long term. Flirting is one thing but bringing her home to see my video games and DnD collection is a totally different story. Girls see the tattoos and piercings and think I'm some badass gangster. I can beat the fuck out of someone- no problem. You can't be as big as I am and be a pussy, but I don't like fighting though. I would way rather cook or be on my gaming system.

I'm not like Clint. I can't walk her through her issues with PTSD, but I can be there for support. Better hurry up and get done then.

It's right at four when I finish up and start getting ready to leave work. I hear a knock at the door and Fletcher is pushing in before I can say come in. "You ready? Holder has to work at the warehouse tonight. So, we don't have to wait on him."

What can I tell him to get out of his party? He isn't one to take no for an answer. "I'm pretty tired. I think I'm gonna skip and go home. Maybe check in on Ayida on the way. It's been a long day."

I don't miss the quirk to his lips when he says,

"Oh? You haven't heard? Ayida is at Clint's. So, if you want to check on her, you'll be going to Clint's anyway."

Fuck it... I'll go and check on her and then head straight home. I get up, stretch and start to leave my desk when I remember what Fletcher said about Holder. "What's Holder doing at the warehouse this late?" Shrugging his shoulders, he leans against the door frame. He looks just like one of the Hollister models, even at almost 30.

"Someone broke in two nights in a row. They fucked up our guys, but didn't steal anything, and you know Holder. If he wants it done right, he'll do it himself." That is curious, but I'm not wasting my Friday night at the warehouse.

We get in his SUV and start the hour-long drive west. It's boring and tedious, but it's worth it. Nothing but trees and more trees for miles. When we pull up to his iron gate you can see the beautiful rolling hills and the old plantation house. Lots of land to ride four-wheelers and horses, and there are ponds for fishing. It's a man's paradise.

Ayida is on the wrap around porch signaling us in with a broad smile and waving arm before we have even parked. She doesn't look like a guest. She looks like she belongs here. She is relaxed with her makeup washed off and her hair up in a messy lopsided bun. She takes off back inside, leaving the door wide open for us. Music is pouring out of the open door and windows. It has a heavy 70s vibe with a good rhythm.

I feel a weight lift off me as I walk up the steps and through the front door. Ayida is dancing around Clint, who is sitting on the couch watching ESPN. I don't know how he can concentrate when she is dancing circles around him swaying her hips and giggling like she is high. Hell, she might be. Clint uses weed to help with his PTSD. It couldn't hurt.

I'm mesmerized when she comes skipping up to me. She is the happiest I've seen her all day. "You want to dance? Clint said he has two left feet. I need a partner." She is pouting in the cutest fucking way. I hate dancing, but I can't tell her no. I don't think I could ever tell her no. She could ask for my heart with those pouty lips and I would pull a "kali ma shakti de" right then and there. Damn I love Indiana Jones.

"Sure… let's see what you got Baby Blue."

Chapter Ten: Ayida

I had a pretty fucked up day. It started off bad and then got worse. Now it is looking up. Clint took control and brought me to his heaven on earth. He said it wasn't much, but this place is gorgeous. I would be okay to never leave... He put on Fortnite, one of the few games I know and let me play around, laugh and just forget for a while. It was just what I needed. He is a special guy for sure. Then he let me know Cole and Fletch were coming over for dinner. I got a little antsy and nervous. To my utter amazement he pulled out a bong from his closet and passed it my way. Now I'm feeling pretty damn good. It's easier to be fun and carefree when you're stoned. Marijuana is not a real drug to me. It's a way to cope with my past. I think it should be legal to help everyone that needs it. My ex is a meth head. Totally different breed than a stoner. A hell of a lot meaner.

Cole spins me and dips me. Makes me feel like a real princess. I didn't see this big tattooed up guy being this graceful and sweet. He flirted at the RV lot, but that's not unusual for me with tattooed guys. I figured he would be a little more standoffish or guarded, but right now he is open and smiling. Skipping around the huge living room and pulling me along with him like a big kid. He is not what I thought. I have to stop judging a book by its cover.

"Dancing is fun, but I think I need to eat. What are we having?" What can I say? I love food.

"We have catfish in the fridge that we just caught this week. Do you know how to make anything?" I know Clint means well, but that just hurt. You can't have my thick ass without knowing how to throw down in the kitchen.

Looking in the fridge I find what I need. "I'll make the coleslaw and fries. Sound good to you, boys?" Cole and Fletch barely nod their heads while trying to kill each other in Mortal Kombat. Men and their toys.

I don't know if I've ever been so turned on while chopping veggies before. Clint decided he needed to take his shirt off so not to get flour on it before he started battering his fish. I use the back of my hand to keep the drool in check. Trying not to cut off my fingers while sneaking peeks at his sculpted back and ass. Damn this man is FINE. I want to lick up his spine starting at the base where his wing tattoos start. I'm not sure if they are angel or demon wings, but they frame his muscular back well. The black ink is like a shadow accentuating the curves and plains. I catch his eyes glancing over his shoulder. Fuck he knows I was watching him like a horny stalker.

I jump back to my task. I drop my cut potatoes

in the hot oil and start on my cabbage when I feel a warm breath on my neck. My first response is to take my knife and slide it backwards into the soft meat between the ribs, but then his rough whisper reminds me I'm not in danger. "Baby Blue, I'm not going to hurt you. I'm just checking your skills out." I relax, but not completely. It's hard to focus when I can feel his hard body just behind me.

"You sure it's my cutting skills you're watching or is it what's down my shirt? 'Because you seem a little close to really appreciate my knife work." I can feel the chuckle before I hear it.

"You caught me. I'm sorry. I couldn't help myself. They are right there and it's hard to find a girl with curves like you." He murmurs in my ear before going back to his task.

It takes a lot for me to get flustered, but something about this big man makes me red and hot all over. He doesn't need to know I want to ride him like a rollercoaster though. He knows he is sexy and that makes it even worse. I love a confident man. He isn't as tatted up as Cole, but he has some ink. The wings on his back, a few words on his ribs. What really catches my eye is a strange tribal style tattoo that starts on his hip and works its way down under his low-slung sweats. I wonder where else that tattoo might travel. My mind slips into dirty mode as I imagine what his hard cock would feel like pressed up against my ass as I stand against the counter. Wondering if it is long and curved or short and wide. I'm getting wet just imagining what he would do if I were to grab him through his pants right now.

Swimming in my lust drunk mind I don't realize my fries are burning until I hear Clint curse. "Fuck, I'm so sorry!" I jump to move the pot off the stove and splash hot oil over my hand. The pain is instant searing heat that feels like the skin is bubbling off. "Shit-muthafucka-damn!" I'm not creative when I'm in pain.

"Baby Blue, let me see." Clint is looming over me with worried eyes. Reaching out to cradle my hands in his huge calloused ones, he gently pulls my unmarred hand off of the burnt one. "Cole, Fletch? Go get my first aid kit!" I'm surprised how loud he can be after he had been so gentle all day.

Leading me to the sink, he runs cold water over the burnt flesh. Instant relief. "I don't know if anyone has told you, but it's a good idea not to let your mind wander while cooking. Even if it's because you're surrounded by all this sexiness." I almost choke on my laugh.

"Full of yourself, aren't we?" He has one sexy smirk that's for sure. Looking up I notice his eyes are on my lips. I can't stop myself. It's like my body is overriding my brain. I step closer pushing my chest flush against his. I bury my nose in the dip at the bottom of his throat. Inhaling his cinnamon scent with a moan. I feel his free hand run up my arm slowly. I'm guessing he doesn't want another incident like earlier today.

My tongue flicks out on its own accord. Tasting the warm salty skin of his throat. I want to taste every inch of him. Hearing the hitch in his breathing makes me smile. After years of being forced to do things, I like being the one leading... for now. I trail my nose up his throat, having to stretch on my tiptoes to reach the helix of his ear. I run the ball of my tongue ring over the sensitive skin. His whole body does a little shiver when I blow on the wetness I left behind. His hand has slid down my side and rests gently on my hip. His fingers kneading the skin softly. I want to touch all of him. Feel his hard body pressed against my soft one. I feel his hardness through his sweats brushing against my stomach. I'm happy to know I'm affecting him the same way he is me.

If he reached down my pants right now, he would come back with a soaked hand. It's been quite a while since I've been this turned on and I have no intention of stopping now. I deserve this after all the bad. A woman should know what a real man feels like. Even if it's just one time. I run my fingers through his soft hair. Massaging his scalp as I pepper kisses over his stubbled jaw and chin. I work up to the corner of his mouth when I finally glance up. Looking at him through my lashes, I can see his stormy blue eyes. He looks hungry, but not for the food we have been working on. I can feel his body tense. I keep my eyes locked with his as I trail the tip of my tongue over his bottom lip. Daring him to take control. Just seeing how far I can push before he loses it.

I'm surprised when he lets me do whatever I want. I nibble his bottom lip and rub my hand over his collarbone and down his chiseled chest and muscled stomach. Stopping at his pants. I glance back up to find he has his eyes closed tightly. He is letting me have all the control and not pushing my boundaries. I think it's time for him to get to explore some. I kiss his lips lightly before taking his bottom lip between my teeth and sucking. When he opens his eyes, I tilt my head giving him access to my throat. Giving him my trust, but cautiously. His eyes light up and his hands climb up my back to press me even tighter to his chest. I feel his hot lips press to my pulse point and his tongue flicks out to taste. BAM! The first aid kit hits the counter beside us.

"What the fuck, dude?" Fletcher and Cole are

back from the basement. "You get her over here, are supposed to take care of her, and you take advantage of her while she's hurt?" Cole's face is red with rage. Honestly, I had completely forgotten the pain with the pleasure pulsing in my clit. Sex is a great pain killer… too bad I didn't get that far. So damn close… fucking cock blocking men!

"I was not taking advantage of anyone! Baby Blue here took it upon herself to rub on me. Not that I minded one damn bit, but y'all should know me better than to think I would do anything she didn't want to do." Clint is fuming now… I guess I'll have to be the referee here.

"Clint isn't lying. I did start everything. I'm sorry to him and to y'all. It's been a long day and my hormones are everywhere. Clint has been so sweet and gentle with me today. I was just enjoying this new kind of attention. I'm sorry for getting in the middle of all this. I'll just head back to Old Man's." I never wanted to get between them. I was just having fun for once. I hate that I messed up the few friends I was making. That's just what's happening though.

I'm about to walk out the kitchen door when Cole puts his hands out in front of him stopping me. "Ayida. We're not mad with you or him. It was just a shock. Please stay." He means it. Fletcher and Clint are nodding along in agreement.

"Well, we were almost done with cooking. I guess I could stay for dinner. As long as y'all are okay with it?" Everyone nods again in unison.

"Can we get your hand fixed up first?" Cole asks from the door. His cheeks stained pink. I'm surprised he is a blusher.

"Thank you. It's starting to throb a little."

Dinner was uneventful. The guys mostly ate in silence after patching up my hand with burn cream and a bandage. If anything, it was awkward. The exact thing I didn't want. "So... What is on the agenda tomorrow?" *Did I mention I suck at small talk?*

"I guess teaching you more about the business. Maybe take you to the bank and get you put on Old Man's accounts. That's important for the days he decides not to show up to the office door." At least

Cole is trying.

"Is this really what we're going to talk about?" I look up to see Clint's narrowed blue eyes looking back and forth between all of us.

"What would you like to talk about, brother?" Fletcher says flippantly. He is trying to aggravate Clint and not hiding it at all.

"Hmmm, maybe how it's none of your business what Ayida does or with whom she does it with?" Tension is rolling off Clint in waves. I'm starting to get nerves building up in my stomach. I might be a badass bitch but arguing makes me anxious. Nothing good ever comes from verbal fighting either. I think Clint can sense my anxiety next to him. Taking a deep breath, he relaxes into his chair and lays his hand on top of mine. "I just mean she shouldn't feel ashamed for anything she does or doesn't do."

Clearing his throat, Cole turns in my direction. "Ayida, you can do whatever you want with whomever you want. We have just met you, and have no claim to you, and should not, and will not judge your decisions. If you like Clint, go for it... if not that's fine too. We are not some backwoods, hillbilly, rednecks that think a woman belongs to a man. We might be criminals, but we aren't sexist." I'm pretty shocked by the openness of his statement. I didn't think they were sexist... assholes maybe, but not sexist. Holder is a different issue all together.

These guys are trying to protect me from

something I don't need protection from. If anything, they need protection from me. I have a dark spot on my soul, and I can feel it growing daily. It will suck in everyone around me eventually. "Well since we're being honest, and everyone is a feminist here. I like all of y'all. Clint was just the one in touching distance when 'la chatte' went all needy and drippy." Cole is bright pink while the other two are choking on laughter.

"That's definitely a first for me. Glad to know I was just a body to rub on." Clint's eyes sparkle with mischief. Okay so not totally true. I do like all three of them, but Clint and I… we click. Who knows, I might click with all them if I get some alone time. They definitely are not lacking in the looks department.

"Okay so you have a thing for all of us. What are we supposed to do with that information? Draw straws?" For being a party boy, Fletcher is sure killing the vibe.

"I don't know, that's up to y'all. I'm not settling down to one person anytime soon. I just got my freedom back and I'm living life to the fullest. If you can't handle that, I'll just cross you off my list of must do's. Cole, you want me to cross you off also or are you cool?" I was expecting to be told "hell no" with all his cute blushing, but to my utter surprise he meets my eyes with confidence.

"I don't mind sharing Blue. I know what I bring to the table." Leaving me with a panty melting smile before returning to his fish. Clint just squeezes my hand and digs into his food. I look up to Fletcher, whose mouth is hanging open, eyes darting back and forth to his friend's heads. His green eyes land on mine.

"Okay so they are cool with sharing apparently. I don't know how to feel about it. I guess I could give it a try. I just don't know what Holder will say to all this." Like I could give two flying fucks what Holder thinks about anything.

"Do y'all have to say anything? He is not my biggest fan if y'all haven't noticed." He is their best friend and I don't want to get between them, but I also don't want him to ruin the first bit of fun I've had in almost a decade.

"He is basically our brother. We don't keep

secrets. That doesn't mean he gets a say in what we do with our free time." Clint doesn't even look up. He is stuffing his face. I think we have an eager beaver on our hands. Now that he has the go ahead, I imagine he'll want to get back to our earlier position as quickly as possible.

"So, how are we going to do this? Timetable of who gets you and when?" Fletcher needs a drink or three.

"Dude, who says we can't share time also? I mean if Baby Blue is good with that too?" Cole is just full of surprises tonight. All heads turn in my direction. No pressure or anything.

"Well, I've never thought much about it. I've never even been on a double date. Hell, you only live once. I can do anything I want, and I want to try everything." Smirks all around. That sounded dirtier than it was meant, and they definitely let their imaginations run with it. "Y'all know what I mean!" Their chuckles warm my heart. It's nice being around nice guys. I feel accepted and like part of the group.

"If everyone is done with dinner, we could go to the movie room and proceed with our first group date?" Clint's wink directed at me makes my belly flutter.

I hope I can handle all this sexiness after all.

Chapter Eleven: Fletcher

I don't know how this even got started. I knew I liked Ayida as soon as she slammed into me at the office, but I was thinking just a little fun. Not a four-way date with my best friends. I'm not saying this isn't fun. Watching a movie and laughing with the neon haired goddess has been a blast. Me and the guys have taken turns seeing who could get her more flustered. So far Cole is a lot better than I thought he would be. He knows exactly what to say to make her squirm. I don't know if I'm ready for the feelings she is causing deep in my chest. Oh well, I'll enjoy the fun and worry about the rest later. It's my time to get Blue to turn pink and shifty. "Baby Blue, how about you come sit with me since these assholes want to tease you so much?"

Her smile lights up her face as she sways her hips walking towards my side of the sectional. The room is dark and warm. The only light is the movie playing in the background. No one is paying it any attention. We have all eyes on her. Stunning. It's almost impossible to breathe when she gets close to me. Her hair smells like chocolate and the heady red wine she was drinking at dinner. I wonder what she smells like between her legs. Other men lie and say women smell like peaches or something equally strange. Women smell like earth. Like dampness and heat. That's what women are when they want you though, hot and wet.

Ayida goes to sit beside me and I snag her hips at the last second depositing her on my lap. Her soft round ass putting pressure on my already tightening pants. Her breath hitches in her chest. I hope I haven't crossed an unseen boundary. She starts to relax, slowly sinking back into my chest. Wrapping my arms around her I rest my hands on her thighs. I look over her shoulder and see my brothers watching every move she makes. Completely enthralled with her body.

"You okay, Blue?" Whispering in her ear so she isn't put on the spot.

"I'm okay. Just a little nervous." She turns her head slightly so I can see her full lips as she whispers back.

"If you ever want to stop just say it. You're in complete control even when we're the ones it seems controlling you. No means no, and we won't cross that line." I kiss behind her ear and earn a shiver.

"Okay just remember I'm still new to all this." She is giving us her trust and we will respect it no matter what.

"We are too, Blue. We'll take care of you. Don't worry, Baby Girl. We'll make sure you have the fun you want."

I use my legs under hers to spread her wide as my hands massage her thighs and hips. Kissing her throat as she lets little moans slip through her beautiful full lips. My hands migrate upwards rubbing under her shirt across the softly rounded plains of her stomach. I move my lips to the shell of her ear, nipping and licking while my hands roam further up. I'm giving her plenty of time to change her mind. So far, I think she is good with everything, if her sounds are any indication. I use one hand to turn her face toward me so I can kiss the corner of her delicious mouth.

My hand finally finds what it's been searching for, but it is covered in a thin satin material. Is that a piercing? I can feel her hard nipple pushing through like it is desperate to be touched. I'm not a tease. Even if I wanted to be, I couldn't be with her. She is like my own personal drug and I want all of it. I run my palm up and over the full globe of her breast and slowly drag it back down trapping her hard, pierced peak between my fingers and gently pull. She gasps and wiggles her ass deeper into my dick. I'm sure she can feel it between her cheeks now.

Grabbing her hips, I spin her around with her thighs pressed on either side of my hips. I grab the hem of her shirt and drag it over her head. Blue hair falling around her like a halo. Her eyes look like fields of green grass speckled with liquid gold. She is staring into mine so intently her pupils seem to dilate. Giving me permission to keep going, no-more like begging. I don't know her story like Clint does, but even I can tell she hasn't been treated like a woman in a long time, if ever.

I grab her sweetheart shaped face and press my lips against hers. Hoping she can feel the truth that this isn't just a fuck. I need this too. Something more than just two bodies grinding together for the pleasure of it. I tilt her head to gain more leverage pushing my tongue against hers in a rough dance. When I pull away, we are both panting. The guys are still watching in complete abandon. Their dicks pressed straight up tenting in their pants. Clint is unashamedly rubbing his cock through his pants. I'm surprised he hasn't tried to take over since he started all this anyway.

Bringing my attention back to the angel in front of me, my eyes go wide as I pull down the cups of her bra and see the little metal bars pierced through those glorious pink nipples of hers. I pinch, twist, and pull her hard peaks before soothing them with my hot mouth.

"Mmmm... Fletch that feels so fucking good," she mumbles. While suckling and licking I feel her hands in my hair and her back starts arching, pressing her chest closer to me as goosebumps erupt as the cool air hits her nipples. I reach around and run my hand up her back until I reach her soft wavy hair. I massage my fingers into her scalp before gathering a handful of her hair to pull and arch her back even more. There is something about her beautiful curvy body pushed flushed against mine.

Kissing up her throat, I slide my free hand down to undo her tight jeans.

I make eye contact with Clint. My hands are too full of flesh to wiggle her pants down her thick ass and thighs, but I'm not about to let her go. Nodding my head down, he understands and hurries over to us and kneels behind her. I feel her tense but kiss her ear. "It's just Clint. I need a little help, Blue. We're not going to do anything you don't want. I promise."

She lets the breath she has been holding go and nods. He reaches for her pants and starts to shimmy them down her luscious hips. She raises one leg at a time for him to wiggle her out of them. When he is done, she is left in nothing but a silver satin thong and the bra that is still pushed below her tits. She is incredible. I could just look at her all night and have a good time. I don't think she, or the guys, would be okay with that being enough though.

Rubbing my hand between her legs and over the soft material I feel her lips swollen and ready. My thick cock throbs beneath her begging for release. I flick my thumb over her needy clit. She jerks, but I still have her long hair wrapped in my hand holding her arched to me. I let my fingers rub slow circles over her clit and back up. Kissing her jaw and chin. Tasting the sweat starting to form. She is squirming like its pure torture, and it's got to be one of the sexiest damn things I've ever seen. I can't help but wonder when the last time was, she got all the attention.

Clint stands behind her rubbing his hands over her ribs and hips holding her, so she doesn't fall off my lap. When he starts kissing her lower back, I can feel her whole-body shake. She is jerking with every kiss and touch. When she is panting and moaning, I slip my fingers under her panties, testing her wet slit. She is soaked and ready. I drive two fingers deep inside her while Clint reaches around to rub her hard nub. It only takes two strokes of my fingers before she is tensing up.

"Oh, my fucking God... what is that? What the ever loving... ughhhh!" Her body goes limp in my lap. My fingers still, clenched by her walls. I slide them out slowly and bring them to my mouth for a quick taste.

Wrapping my arms around her, I kiss her neck and chest, and I pick her up and tote her up the stairs to Clint's room. My hard-on is painfully pressed to my zipper. Clint and Cole follow close behind me. I lay her on the king size bed covered in soft furry blankets and pillows. Her body is covered in a sheen of sweat and her chest is rising quickly with each breath. Her eyes are hooded and watching every move I make as I slip off her bra and panties.

"You ready for the rest of us, Baby Blue?"

Chapter Twelve: Ayida

Am I ready? I just had an orgasm so powerful I thought my vagina might just implode. I've had small orgasms by myself, but nothing like that ever! It was mind and soul blowing. My legs are still tingling and floppy. I didn't think I would ever want a man to take control again but having someone bring you indescribable pleasure without having to ask, was world changing. I felt like a goddess being worshipped by two beautiful men. Now there are three standing in front of me looking like gods themselves. My legs spread wide, my wetness coating my thighs. I feel empowered. They would do anything I asked right now. Fuck it. As the saying goes, "Laissez le bon temps rouler" and I'm ready to get MY good times rolling- starting right now...

"I want Cole to lick me clean." Where the fuck did that come from? I've never been the pushy kind in bed. Maybe it's time things change. I deserve what I want.

"I can do that." He smiles so innocently at me. Long lashes feathering his cheeks as he kneels between my legs at the end of the bed. Right before his tongue darts out, his eyes meet mine and I realize he is far from innocent. He has the look of the devil right before he pushes his tongue between my folds and zeros in right on my aching clit. Electricity shoots up my spine as I dig my fingers into the blankets.

"Clint, you want to show her what your tongue can do up here?" Fletcher taunts as he plucks one nipple between his fingers seemingly entranced by my adornments.

All the sensation has me pushing my heels into the bed and my back bowing. Not for long though. Cole has my legs pushed up and settles my thighs on his shoulders. He uses his fingers to pull me apart and dives his tongue into my core before lapping at my swollen clit again.

Clint's handsome face appears in my blurry vision. Pressing his firm lips to mine, the rough stubble on his jaw adds another sensation to the myriad I'm already feeling. His big hand palms one breast while the other digs into the thick hair at the back of my head. Pulling my lips even closer. Inhaling every moan and scream before I can even hear them. I feel eyes watching me. It's not without difficulty, but I manage to drag my eyes open.

Fletcher is laying behind my head, stretched out, lazily stroking his hard cock. His teasing smile and dimpled cheeks send even more flutters to my belly. Licking my lips and building up my courage I try to reach for him, my mouth salivating for a taste. Sliding closer he nudges Clint's hip. Clint doesn't even question it. For this to be their first time doing this they act like a well-oiled machine. Makes me wonder what they are like together at work. Doing all the stuff no one wants to show me... all the things I'm the most curious about.

Clint moves down to kiss and caress my breasts, suckling my pierced nipples, and leisurely trails his tongue down my ribs distracting me from my wandering thoughts. He circles my navel and back up again. Fletcher gives me that sexy dimpled grin of his when I gasp as Cole hits a certain spot with his fingers, while sucking my clit better than any Hoover ever could. I feel like a tight wind-up toy that is ready to spring into action any minute. Fletcher grabs my hair like he did before, tilting my chin up to kiss me slowly.

"Open up Blue. Let's see how dirty we can get you." When I open my eyes the smooth bulbous head of his glorious cock is at my lips. This I know how to do. I can suck the chrome off a trailer hitch. I might not have received much pleasure the last few years, but I was basically trained in giving great head. Firmly grabbing his cock, I let his precum paint my lips before I lick off the wetness. He tastes even more delicious than I imagined. I then let my jaw go slack and open wide. He is pretty fucking big. Not overly long, but thick enough to make my jaw stretch. Sliding in until he reaches the back of my throat, I lock my lips around the base and suck. Bobbing my head, the best I can while on my back;

he leans over me slightly to angle it even deeper. I relax as much as I can while Cole is still eating my wet cunt like it's his last meal, and Clint has my taut nipple between his teeth and tugs the bar, holding my hands to my sides keeping me from reaching out. Pleasure mixed with pain.

Why is it so damn hot to be deep throated and owned by three men after everything I've been through? I don't know, but fuck if I'm not about to have the biggest orgasm of my life. It's almost like they are telepathic. Cole and Clint bite me gently, but hard enough to sting right when Fletcher shoves in as far as he can go and shoots his thick ropes of cum down my greedy throat. All my muscles clench and release in rhythm. I then cum hard in Cole's mouth. I know because he is lapping and moaning, cleaning up every drop like he can't get enough.

"God damn Baby Girl! I think that's the best head I've ever had. I wasn't planning on finishing that way. I had bigger plans for you, but when that tongue ring rolled over my shaft, I was a goner." Looking slightly disappointed, he tilts my head back and open mouth kisses me slowly, deeply, and thoroughly like he is savoring his salty taste on my tongue.

"We have plenty of time to go for round two. I still have these two big guys to give me more earth shattering orgasms. I'll have my hands full for a little bit." Smirking he kisses me again and scoots back up the bed, waiting to watch the show that is about to start.

Clint works his way back up to his previous spot now that it's been vacated. Kissing my jaw and working up to my ear, "That looked like one hell of a blowjob, Blue. I might need to see what that mouth can do here soon, but first I'm going to hold your knees to your head so Cole can drive into you so fucking hard and deep you're going to be walking funny tomorrow. I know you're a tough one and can handle a hard fuck, right?" Clint must be some kind of pussy whisperer because just his words are causing moisture to build back up between my thighs.

I glance down between my legs and see Cole standing with his dick, long, hard and curving upwards slightly, in his fist slow stroking it. It's massive, just like he is. He gives me that devil-may-care smile again. He knows it, Clint knows it, Fletch knows it and now I know it. He is about to wreck me in every delicious way. His muscles were intimidating to begin with but now, looking at them, it sends a thrilling shiver through my body. "I love it rough, but just remember what I've shared with you. I do have boundaries and some hard-no-go lines." I plead with my eyes. I do want it rough, fast, and raw after all the work up I've had from these men, but I also don't want to end up a whimpering puddle when this is all over.

"Baby Girl, the moment you say 'no' is the moment it all stops. You are in charge 100 percent. If you want to stop now, we'll understand." Oh, hell no! I didn't come this far to stop now. I've been a caged animal all this time and it's time I get to do what I want.

"No. I want this. I want y'all. Let's do this!"

Chapter Thirteen: Cole

She is so fucking beautiful laying there spread out naked and bare for us. I could worship every inch of her, but right now I'm going to give her the hard ride she so desperately needs. I grab her thick thighs and drag her closer to the edge of the bed. Clint making his way to her head, grabs her knees and hoists them up and closer to her shoulders. All I can concentrate on is the pale pink skin of her beautiful pussy and that soft round ass. I would love nothing more than to spank that smooth flesh and turn it red with one hand while wrapping my free hand around her long length of hair and pulling on it like my own fuck-me handle. Not now though. That has to wait for a discussion first. Right now, I'm about to drive her to heaven… or maybe hell who knows.

Bracing one hand on the back of her thigh I grab my straining cock. It feels like it just might explode at any second, so I quickly line it up with her opening. "Deep breaths, beautiful." Looking up she has her eyes wide open and focused on the spot where we are about to join. Her tongue darts out wetting her lips.

She replies simply, "Yes, Sir." and I drive in all the way nudging her cervix. *Oh, my own nickname-I like that!* Her eyes roll back, and her mouth opens in a silent scream as her legs begin to shake again. Getting comfortable and letting her adjust is almost impossible. She is hot, wet, and soft. Her slickness coats my shaft like silk. Her walls clamp down on me and I want to pound into her over and over. I'll get my chance, but first I have to make sure she is okay.

"Blue? How are we doing?" After what feels like minutes, she finally opens her eyes, draws in a ragged breath, and gives me a 100-watt smile.

"Fuuuuck! We are really good. Let's see what that dick can do."

Challenge accepted. Pulling almost all the way

out slowly I drive back into her sweet cunt until I bottom out. Her whole-body tensing around me. I could fuck this woman every day and never get tired of her. I drive back in six more times before I'm about to explode in her. "Okay so we either need to switch positions or I'm going to have to tap out. Your cunt is fucking magic." I'm not insecure. I can admit when I'm going to finish too soon and know how to fix it. Before I can say anything, else Clint has flipped Ayida over on her belly. That perfect ass in my face taunting me. "I don't know how long I can last like this either, but it's worth a shot."

Grabbing a handful of her soft ass cheek and kneading it. "Don't worry about it, bud. What you don't do, I will." Clint says with a chuckle. He pulls her up on her elbows and knees doggy-style before shucking his pants and throwing them off the bed.

"I want both of y'all. One in my mouth and one buried deep in my pussy. I'm aching for it." She says on a half moan as Clint tweaks her nipples again, pulling on her small metal bars.

"Damn Blue. Are you trying to get me to cum on this beautiful ass right now?" Before she can say another word, I drive home again. Pushing her forward and right into Clint's crotch. He grabs his cock and feeds it to her while I start a fast punishing pace from behind. Bracing myself with her wide hips, I cherish her wet channel hugging me in every spot. I hear her muffled moans, but all I can see are Clint's hands running circles over her head and shoulders with his eyes clenched shut, as she devours his length.

Alternating between deep slow strokes and short fast strokes it doesn't take long for her body to start spasming around me. I hear her whimpers while Clint takes over the work of fucking her mouth in sync with me. Feeling a gush of warm silky liquid around my cock is enough to send me over the edge. I pull out right at the last second and spray her back with rope after rope of my seed. Finally coming back to reality, I let go of her hips to see finger shaped bruises forming.

I hear Clint grunting. Apparently, her blowjobs are that good. He is holding her head carefully as his body goes tense and his mouth drops open with a husky moan. Well I think he finished differently than he wanted to.

Getting up slowly to go clean up and grab a towel, I see Fletch has already gotten one and is cleaning Ayida's back off. Heading to the bathroom to get fully clean myself I hear Fletcher speaking soothingly to her. He is good at this part. The part I'm awkward at. The hormones and endorphins start to settle and I'm not sure what to do. Clint and Fletch will take care of her. I'll grab a shower and she'll either be asleep or on her way home when I get out.

It's for the best.

Chapter Fourteen: Ayida

Holy flying fuck! My body is charged like I touched a live wire. I still have Clint's salty taste in my mouth as Fletcher rubs soothing hands over my shoulders, down my back and legs. Clint massages my scalp and hums a tune that is familiar, but I can't quite pin down.

Wow. The sex was amazing, but the after treatment is life changing. I've never been pampered like this. A girl could and will get used to feeling cherished. "So Blue, how was your first time with multiple men? As good as you hoped or still needs work?"

I know where Fletcher is going. I don't care that we only made it through two positions before the guys blew their loads in me and on me. Hell, before now I was lucky to get any attention really. An orgasm was basically a thing of legends. "It was amazing. Every minute was perfect."

I squirm deeper into the soft blankets like I'm making a nest. Hearing the bathroom door open stops me. Cole is peeking out and looks somewhat crestfallen seeing me still in the bed. My heart aches at the thought. Reminding myself I already said this was "no strings attached" fun; I push the feelings aside. "I can go home if y'all are ready for bed." I move to get up, but Fletcher grabs my waist.

"You ain't going anywhere, Baby Blue, unless you want to. We're happy with you right here." Damn there is that warm fuzzy feeling I was getting with Clint earlier. I can't get wrapped up in feelings with these men. I have issues to take care of before I can settle down with anyone.

"You want a drink before we lay down? I'm getting a beer. Helps me sleep." Clint asks before heading to the door. I guess I'll take that as a formal request to stay the night.

"A water would be nice. Thank you." Cole is heading for the door as well. Calling up my inner bitch I decide he isn't getting out of here without at least a goodbye. "And where the fuck do you think you're going? Fucking and ducking I see." He stops dead in his tracks.

"What? No! I just figured y'all had a bed full, and you have made it known this is fun only. I was just gonna borrow one of Clint's cars and go home since my motorcycle isn't here." He looks down sheepishly. He thinks I don't want him…

"Get the fuck over here. This bed is big enough for everyone unless you're worried, you'll wake up with one of their hard-ons up your ass?" Fletcher cackles openly at that. Swinging his head up to look at me, his cheeks that adorable pink again, he scoots his way closer to the bed and undresses with his back to me before climbing under the blankets and sliding behind me.

"Where the fuck am, I supposed to sleep? Y'all are in my damn bed and I got to sleep on the edge!" Clint is standing at the door looking thoroughly pissed.

"Shouldn't have went to get that beer, Sir." Fletcher just lives to tease and taunt.

Raising his eyebrows and nodding Clint sits the drinks on the dresser and launches himself across the bed tackling Fletcher and pushing him out of the bed with a triumphant "Fuck you!" Cole grabs me and pulls me to his chest to keep me away from the wrestling friends. I turn towards him and bury my face in his tattooed chest. Inhaling his smell of soap and a brand-new book scent.

That's the last thing I remember before waking up in a dark room.

Chapter Fifteen: Clint

What the fuck is that sound? My ears are bleeding. Sitting up in bed as fast as humanly possible I notice the whole bed is jerking and jumping. Scrubbing my eyes as best I can I see Cole holding a screaming convulsing Ayida. "What the fuck is going on? Is she okay?" It only takes me a few seconds to recognize the night terror. Fletch is now up and leaning over Cole trying to sooth the terrified girl.

I run my hands over her back and speak in a calm low voice. "Shhh. It's okay Baby Blue. We're here. You're safe." After a few minutes she finally calms down and is somehow still sleeping. Sweat coats her forehead and chest.

"We have to do something. It's not right. She needs help." Fletcher has good intentions, but it can be hard to hear that you need professional help from other people. A lot of PTSD victims brush it off and try to suffer in silence. It feels like admitting weakness to search out help.

"We'll discuss it in the morning. Right now, we have... maybe 2 hours of sleep left. Let's make the best of it. Hand her over, Cole." He looks unsure, but scoots Ayida over towards my side of the bed. "Y'all get some sleep. I'm just going to watch and make sure she is good and asleep before I lay back down." Sometimes you can have aftershocks from a night terror. I've been known to sleepwalk after having one. "Goodnight," both guys look exhausted.

I'm waking up to bright sunlight pouring in through the open curtains. "Who the fuck opened the curtains?" Huffs the little Blue Demon next to me while yanking the blankets up over her head. Peeking underneath I see hair sticking out in directions that defy gravity. I can't even make out her face with all the hair hiding her from my view. She is truly rumpled and twisted up now, but still so picturesque I can't help but feel a slight jump from my dick.

"Blue, you probably want to go get a shower. I think your hair has taken on a life of its own and is trying to smother you to death." The kick to my shin was probably deserved, but I thought a joke would help her morning personality.

"Fuck you and your shower. " She grumbles burrowing further into the blankets like a mole.

"I'll fuck you in the shower if that's what you want Blue." My dick twitches at the mention of fucking her. I didn't get my turn with her pussy, but if it's anything like that sassy mouth it wouldn't take me long to mark her with my cum.

"Ugh, I'm fairly certain I seized the wrong day," she muttered. "Coffee. If you want to live another minute. I need coffee. Where are the other asshats?" It takes her asking for me to start wondering the same. I jump out of bed. Well more like a slow bounce. I'm stiff as hell after sleeping with the kicking queen on top of me. She beats ass even in her sleep. "Black." Her cute head pops out from the blankets. "Just like my soul. Thanks!" Well that was a switch. I guess coffee is her drug of choice.

Heading downstairs I smell the bacon and coffee before I get to the kitchen. Baby Blue will be pleased with her offerings. "Is the she-devil awake yet?" Fletcher chuckles while giving me a once over.

"She is demanding sustenance." Cole gets a laugh from that one while filling up a plate with bacon and a mug of black coffee. "Let's all go pay our respects to the Blue Demon." This nickname thing is getting fun. I can't wait for her to hear them.

Smiling to myself, I head back up with her nourishment. She is leaning back on all the pillows looking adorably disheveled. " We have brought your offerings."

Her brows arch up to her hairline. "I want to cuss at all of y'all, but I smell bacon and coffee. So, I'll let it slide. Gimme!" Laying the plate of bacon down and passing her the mug, I notice how her eyes light up. I don't think she has ever had someone take care of her. Every time someone does the smallest thing, she acts like they have given her the moon. She dives for the bacon like a wild animal. It doesn't take her long to polish off every bit of what we brought up.

"So Blue, we were wanting to talk about last night."

Her eyes dim at Fletcher's statement. I rush to correct her assumption. "Not what we did last night. What happened after you fell asleep." Her eyebrows draw up in confusion. "Last night, well really early this morning you had a night terror and scared the shit out of all of us." Reaching for her hand and stroking her palm, I ask the questions I was once asked. "Did you know about them? Have you seen anyone about what you've been through?" Fletcher and Cole have suspicions but have not been told the whole story and that's up to her. It's only her story to tell.

"I'm so sorry. I didn't know they had got that bad. I haven't talked to anyone about them. I don't like shrinks." Her beautiful eyes well up, but she holds the tears at bay.

"Baby Blue, seeing a therapist is not as taboo as you think. I've been seeing one for years and it has helped a ton." I want to put her at ease, but I know as well as anyone how people can feel right after suffering the kind of trauma she has. You definitely don't want to relive every minute with a stranger.

"I'll think about it. I won't sleep here anymore. I don't want to disturb y'all." She really doesn't understand what we're trying to do. I'm guessing she hasn't had many friends over the last five years either.

"Baby Blue, you are welcome here anytime. Last night was fun, but if you don't want to do it again, we will all understand, and we will still be here for you. That's what friends do." Her smile and watery eyes break my heart.

"Group hug!" Cole grabs everyone with his thick arms and squishes us together in the middle of the bed. The snorting laugh coming from the Blue Demon makes me chuckle.

I have a feeling thing are about to get really interesting.

Chapter Sixteen: Clint

And interesting it has been. It's been 2 weeks since the Blue Demon waltzed into our lives and it's been nothing but craziness ever since. She spends the weekends at my place with me, Cole and Fletch, just having a good time playing video games, cooking together, and trying as many sexual positions in as many rooms as we can. She is sweet and withdrawn one minute, and then the next she is jumping down someone's throat. Usually that's Holder though.

He refuses to even acknowledge her anymore. He isn't particularly fond of us either. He views getting involved with Ayida as professional suicide. I see it as the most fun I've had in a long fucking time. Her night terrors are still horrible, and if she is in Old Man's house or mine by herself, and someone comes in or surprises her she goes into full attack mode and then deals with the guilt afterwards.

Today, I'm going to help that... I hope.

Pulling into the sanctuary, with Fletcher in the passenger seat, I'm nervous. I hope this is the right decision. "Dude, have you seen pictures or anything yet or are we going into this blind?" He seems nervous too. We're already here so might as well go through with it.

"Let's just see how it goes. It could be exactly what she needs." Probably should have asked her first, but it's easier to beg forgiveness than ask permission.

Walking to the door I hear a lady yelling for everyone to "Shut the fuck up!" Great sign... I can feel Fletch sigh and shake his head.

"This is just brilliant. You are gonna get us beat the fuck up. I can see it now. Ayida is going to string us up by our balls and use us like pinatas." He is being very over dramatic today. I blame it on all the sex and not enough sleep. Before we can knock the door swings open and a tiny old wrinkled woman, with gray dreads and huge square glasses, is standing in front of us with a glare that must be permanent.

"About time! Take this fucker before I use him for a stew," she gestures her gnarled fingers to a covered object on a table just inside the door. Jerking off the blanket, she reveals the ugliest fucking bird I've ever seen. Its feathers are extremely thin throughout; it must have plucked itself almost clean. So, this pitiful thing is more skin than anything else. Its creepy eyes make me feel like he is staring a hole into my soul.

"What the hell is that?" Fletcher screeches, jumping back like the bird might attack. Getting right to the point like usual.

"That is what y'all are here for. Meet Donut, your new alert bird. You're welcome! Thank you for coming, goodbye!"

She tries handing me the cage with the strange alien looking creature, but I sidestep her and put my hands up to block any future attempts. "Ain't no way in hell we are bringing that thing anywhere! It looks like something already ate it and coughed it back up."

Fletcher, turning to leave, throws up a peace sign before heading back to my car. That just leaves me and the old hippie. Luckily for her I was raised a little more polite than Fletcher, and the Navy taught me even more respect. Fucking Navy and good upbringing.

"Look, this is not the bird I thought I was getting. I was thinking of a beautiful, colorful, friendly looking parrot. This bird is gray and looks like he might survive on the souls of his enemies. The exact opposite of my criteria. The bird I need is going to a girl with severe PTSD and it needs to be like an emotional support animal that can also alert her to intruders. I mean he looks scary enough to keep anyone out, but that's about it. I'm gonna have to keep looking."

The old woman makes a grab for my hand and is faster than I anticipated. "If you don't take this bird he is going to have to be put down. I'm old and can't handle this many birds. I'm a rescuer. I get birds all the time in bad shape. With the right love and care he'll be beautiful again in no time. Maybe that's what she needs. A project to put love into. Y'all are his last hope. Don't you believe in second chances? Because that is what this bird needs..." Her wrinkled fingers digging into my hand in desperation.

Damn it… she is good. I take one more look at the hideous creature. Huddled down in the cage, he does look sad, I hate for any animal to be put down unless it absolutely has to be. Ugh… I can't believe this. "Are you sure he can alert?" Her eyes grow huge behind her odd glasses. She knows she has won.

"Oh yes! He is an exceptionally good alert bird.

He won't let anyone in without you knowing it. Scout's honor." She says holding up three fingers. She was probably born before the scouts had even started.

I harrumph, rubbing my tired face. I reluctantly reach out for the cage. The old woman almost looks giddy with dare I say a twinkle in her eye. "Like I was saying, his name is Donut and he is an African grey parrot. He has a slight anxiety issue. That's why he is losing feathers. I'm sure when he gets to his new home, he'll be fine and back to normal quickly. His last owner was an older gentleman and sadly passed away leaving Donut alone, but he is very smart and learned a lot from his previous owner. I'm sure y'all will get along fine, you'll see!" She rambles on with more info as she gets a bag together with food and other necessities.

Before I know it, I'm pushed out the door and walking back to my car to an utterly shocked Fletcher. "What the fuck man? Do you even have balls? All you had to say was no thanks and walk out, but somehow you leave with that fucking goblin?" I just shrug and buckle Donut's cage in the back seat.

"Everyone deserves a second chance, right Fletcher?" I smile smugly crossing my arms and glancing back at Donut.

"I guess, but why did it have to be us?" He grumbles.

"We're doing a good thing. It's about time to balance the scales from all the bad we've done. It's time for some good karma." I crank the car, and I start to drive away when I hear Donut finally moving around and making some little chirping sounds. Maybe Blue will like him after all.

"Get the fuck out of my house! Out fucker-out fucker!" Donut squawks from the back seat.

"... Fuck me."

Chapter Seventeen: Holder

What is it with these idiots? Fawning all over Ayida like they do. Yes, I'll admit she is beautiful, sassy and funny. She is going to ruin them. You can't have a woman like her in this life. We don't need love; we need women that will listen and obey. You can always get your sexual needs satisfied elsewhere. You can't lead a Family like this and be head over heels for a girl. Your enemies will use that against you. Hell, she could use that against us. They would do anything she asked.

"Cole, are you going to come help at the warehouse tonight? I need to go take care of some stuff and need you there." Glancing his way, I can't help but notice his fingers flying over his phone screen. Good grief. I bet he is texting her again. "Cole! Are you listening?" Slinging his head in my direction, he gives me a sheepish grin.

"Sorry. Fletcher and Clint are wanting to give Ayida her surprise, but I want to see it first. I'm trying to convince them to wait till tomorrow so I can be there. I'll watch the warehouse tonight, but only till 2 a.m. then you'll have to find a replacement. I got to get some sleep. Ayida has been keeping us busy and I'm exhausted." He ends on a wink.

What the actual fuck is going on? Was she just named after a Vodou deity or does she possess the powers of one in her pussy too? She has them wrapped. Talk about putting a pussy on a pedestal. It can't be that good, can it? "Whatever. I'll be back by then. You can do what you want after that." I'm sure it sounds like I'm whining and probably even jealous, but it's more than that. I'm worried about my brothers. They have never been this involved with a girl. Her being Old Man's girl is worse. They don't take that old codger seriously enough. I mean I kill people and like it. He kills people and loves it. I probably would too if the worry of being found out by my brothers didn't damper the festivities. In our lifestyle you have to be ready for violence. We deal with too many dangerous people not to be.

It's 5pm I have time to drop Cole off with his motorcycle, get home, change, and make it to the meeting spot in time. Turning on to Cole's street, I see him texting away again. Ugh... I just want to snatch his phone and throw it out of the window. "I'll see you at 2 or maybe before if I get done quickly. Do not leave until I get back. I don't trust anyone else but us right now."

Opening the door, he nods, but I'm not sure he

is paying attention. "I know, I know. I'll be waiting. Just because you think something is going on doesn't mean we all do." He says, shaking his head. Closing the door before I can get out a retort. He makes his way to the warehouse building entrance and disappears. When did it get to the point, we talk to each other like this? Is she really driving us apart, or am I?

I get home earlier than expected, but even though I would love a shower it's better to wait till after I'm done. After changing into plain gray sweats and throw away shoes, I lock up and leave. Heart beating in a jarring rhythm I drive to the marina with faint tension in my shoulders cementing my somber mood. Anyone looking would see a pretty rich boy in a nice car going to check on his yacht. If they decided to look closer, they would see a bag filled with tools and weapons that would make Guantanamo Bay prisoners flinch.

This is my specialty. I don't fear anyone. The others couldn't handle this, so the first time we got an assignment of information retrieval I took it. I always knew I was darker and more twisted than my brothers. Always curious about how things work and how people make decisions. Does fear of pain influence people more than the pain itself? What about fear for your loved ones? Is it a stronger motivator than fear for yourself? I ask the hard questions and I love doing the research.

Making my way to the yacht named after my mother, "The Working Girl," I can already hear muffled voices inside. "Boss, how's it going?" Bastien echoes from the deck.

"What have I said about smoking on my yacht?" His eyes bulge as he flips his cigarette onto the pier below, adjusts his cufflinks like a nervous tic, and backs farther away from me.

"Sorry Boss. My nerves were gettin' the best of me. Augustine is inside with the package." Nodding my acknowledgement, I take the steps two at a time going down into the living quarters. The big burly Augustine is standing in front of the bathroom door.

"Boss, the package is ready and waiting like you requested." His head bowing in respect, or fear. I don't quite care which one. Sliding the door open I find my prize. Two weeks of guarding the warehouse

I finally caught one of the subordinates that's been fucking up my business. Never stealing just causing a fuss and tearing shit up. I'm about to find out why.

He is duct taped to a thin metal chair in the tiny shower. His eyes are even duct taped closed along with his mouth. The smell of urine and fear permeates the small room. "Well I'm sure you know why you're here so let's get to it. Shall we?" Ripping off the eye covering and taking some of the sensitive skin with it. The chair wobbles as he fights against his restraints. "So, let's just get to the nitty-gritty of it. Why was you at my warehouse and who sent you? And don't lie. I know it wasn't your idea. You're the muscle, not the brains, that's easy enough to see." He was muscular, but even he couldn't handle the baton against the head. He went down like a sack of bricks.

Jerking off the tape attached to his mouth, I smirk and show him the pliers in my grip. "I don't know who sent me. He paid in an envelope dropped off at a bar. The money was split between me and three other guys. I just did it for the money. Please, let me go and you won't ever see me again!" The tears and snot are almost enough to make me believe him, but guys like this idiot would seek revenge. He would search me out and try and hurt me. He wouldn't succeed, but he might hurt someone else in the process.

"How were you contacted?" Holding his fingers in my hand, I listen and watch for any of the signs of deception. Darting eyes, higher pitched voice, heavy breathing.

"The bartender had been asking around. I needed the money, so I volunteered. I figured I wasn't really hurting anyone. Just aggravating more than anything. Please, that's all I know- please let me go!"

No signs of lying, but I also feel he isn't saying everything. I use the pliers and grab the tip of his pinky finger. "You sure you don't have anything else to say? Anything at all? Something slipping your mind?" I say while applying pressure and bending his digit backwards towards his wrist.

"NO! What the fuck man? I don't know! Please! Don't do this!" I can feel his tendons snapping making my heart speed up.

How can I love to cause this much pain in my work, but crave being submissive during sex? Not just sex, but in a relationship, or whatever you want to call what I have with the women I employ. There is seriously something twisted up inside me... could Blue ever embrace me with this darkness?

Shaking out that thought, and coming back to the task at hand, I finish off snapping his finger backwards. It breaks the cartilage and tendons holding his finger together. It is so interesting figuring out what works best for each person when it comes to pain. Screaming surrounds me. "Are we ready to communicate better now?" I smile in his screaming face.

"Okay, okay, okay! I swear the only thing I know

is I heard the bartender talking to someone on the phone the last time I went to pick up my share. She said, 'Once the Family was busy dealing with the warehouse problems, it would be easy to take the blue-haired bitch.'"

My heart stops. There can only be one blue-haired bitch. Not saying blue hair is super rare in Louisiana, but she is the only one associated with the Family. Not having time to play with my prize, I unsheathe my Benelli and deliver a quick, silent shot to his brain stem. I need to find my brothers.

Ayida Underhill has brought disorder to the Family and I have to remedy the situation- stat.

Chapter Eighteen: Ayida

"What are y'all asshats hiding?" I am not a patient person. Wrapping my arms around Clint, usually the first to give in. "Pleassseee! I don't do well with surprises if you haven't noticed." Batting my lashes as best I can. God knows I'm not an overly feminine woman.

"Sorry Baby Blue. Cole specifically asked to be here when we reveal our grand plan. He'll be here either late tonight or in the morning. You can survive." Grabbing my arms and spinning me so my back is against his chest.

"We can help take your mind off of everything." Fletcher murmurs against my ear. Instructing Clint to hold my arms behind my back, Fletch, dragging this lip down my throat, and slides my gray tube top down over my tits.

My pierced nipples tingle and harden from the cold air coming from the vent above us. His mouth latches on to one pert tip as his fingers graze the crotch of my flimsy pajama shorts. My breath hitches in my chest feeling Clint's cock nestled in my ass crack. Even with all the sex we've been having I still haven't had anyone near my back entrance. I'm very curious though. A little pain with pleasure makes it even better. Biting and licking on my full breasts, Fletcher works my clit through the thin fabric until I'm begging him for more. Clint's mouth is hot and wet on my throat, but his big hands still hold me in a locked position. Jerking and squirming against his hold I feel so close to release only for Fletch to remove his fingers. "I'll be good. I'll be good. Please! I was so close!"

Fletcher's teasing smile comes from below as he drops to his knees. Clint's foot pushes my legs further apart from behind. Sliding my shorts to the side, he runs a finger through my slickness and tastes it. My whole body wants to go slack. If it wasn't for Clint I would have already tackled Fletch and rode his face until he drowned in my cum. Pulling my shorts off completely, I feel his breath on my pussy right before he sucks my clit in between his teeth. Jerking in reaction, but unable to go anywhere, I let out a low throaty moan. His sucking and nibbling are driving me skyward. Submerging two of his fingers, knuckle deep, has me writhing against Clint in desperation.

So close... repeats in my mind. His fingers curl in a come here motion and that's it. I'm gone- rocketing into space. Fireworks shoot off behind my eyelids. He works my pussy with his mouth and fingers until I can hardly move. Just a dead weight in Clint's arms. Coming up from the ground with a drenched face and a smile, Fletch reaches out, barely putting his hand against my throat and leans into me, whispering in my ear, "That's a good girl."

I might be fucked in the head for liking this after everything I've been through, but no one has ever looked at me or treated me the way these men do. I'm learning you can have freedom and still be owned.

Chapter Nineteen: Ayida

Waking to whispering coming from beside the bed is not a good feeling. My nerves shoot up, but I stay completely still. Shock overtakes me when I recognize Holder's voice. What is he doing here? What are they talking about? Staying as silent as possible I turn my head towards them to get a better listen.

"I have a fairly good idea who might be wanting to get to her. Y'all know she doesn't like talking about her past unless she has to. Her night terrors and PTSD are caused by her abusive ex. If you would have took the time to get to know her, Holder, you would know he held her captive for days without food, beat on her, repeatedly forced himself on her, berated her, and caused all the trauma she deals with now." Clint states poignantly.

"My best guess would be its him causing the problems. The only issue with my theory is she described him as a meth head with no job or money. He stole anything he wanted or needed. So how could he pay these idiot mercenaries to do all the shit they have been doing?" Hearing Clint explain my situation to Holder makes my stomach churn. I don't want pity from that asshole. He made sure to stay away from me and only gives me hateful looks when we do cross paths. The last thing I want is sympathy from him.

"I get it. She is damaged goods so y'all treat her like a porcelain doll, but her being here is messing up everything. Not just the business, but our lives and friendship. I'm trying to keep us on track and she just keeps pushing us off course," Holder scoffs.

That's it I can't lay here and listen to anymore. My rage has built until it feels like fire under my skin. "Please explain to the class exactly how I'm messing up your life? I would love to know! I haven't done anything to you. You're the one that refuses to come around your friends just because they have a girlfriend." Stopping abruptly, I look around waiting for someone, anyone to correct my mistake. I am not their girlfriend. I am a friend with benefits, at most, and I don't need to get that mixed up.

"Exactly! It's almost like you don't want us to be happy, Holder! We finally have a girlfriend, one that we share and brings us closer together and instead of trying to be her friend or at least polite, you have done nothing but pull away from us and be mean to her. Are you sure you're worried for us or really just worried you're going to be alone while we're happy together?" Holder and my head both jerk in Cole's direction.

My words caught in my throat. Did he really just say it? Looking around at the others, they seem good with the label. We'll have this conversation later. Right now, I have to tear Holder a new one.

Before I can open my mouth Fletch decides to put his two cents in. "For fuck's sake. We do not treat her like a doll. Far from it. She is strong and wild. She doesn't need protection. She can take care of herself. We just give her all the attention she deserves. What's wrong with caring for someone and showing them that you appreciate them? I know you don't know what a relationship is supposed to look like. You've had horrible examples in your life, but what we are doing with Blue is our normal. Maybe you should try not being an asshole to women for once and see what it's like. You might enjoy what happens."

My mind is left reeling. They all care for me. They appreciate me. It's hard to stay mad with Holder when these hunky sweet guys are saying all the right things. Wait why is he even here? My emotions have gotten the best of me and I forgot to ask what was going on.

"Why the fuck are you even here in the middle of the night?" Feeling a cool breeze, I remember I'm completely naked under the thin sheet. Clutching it closer to my body does little to ease my red cheeks and only serves to draw Holder's attention to my trembling hand. His eyes glued to me has me a little on edge. He looks like he wants to kiss me, but at the same time drive me out to the middle of nowhere and leave me for the animals. That's a lot to get from someone's expression, but Holder has very telling eyes.

"Holder? What cha looking at? You gonna tell the beautiful Blue why you're here at 3 a.m. or do we have to?" Fletcher taunts. Causing Holder to swing his attention back to the guys.

"I'm pretty sure we know what he was looking at. He claims he doesn't like Ayida and wants her gone, but I've never seen him look at any girl the way he just did her. Holder here has a crush and is mad at himself for it. So, like a big man-child, he is taking it out on everyone else. Jealous prick." Clint hit the nail on the head apparently because Holder is turning red and won't look at me. I'm sure he can feel my stare and probably hear my heavy breathing.

"I don't have a crush. I'm not a gottdamn teenager. I'm here to warn my best friends that this girl is going to ruin everything we have worked for because she brought her stupid problems with her."

"What are you talking about?" My heart is pounding like a jackhammer trying to escape my chest. My hands are clammy, apparently stealing all the moisture from my mouth. I had nightmares of this moment, but I had hoped my ex was smart enough to leave well enough alone.

"Someone is using decoys to mess with our warehouse and cause problems as a distraction to try and get to you. They know they can't just come straight at you. Old Man would never let that shit fly. If they cause a big enough issue the majority of our men will have to be stationed at the warehouse, and that leaves you an open target when you're not surrounded by these idiots," Holder spits out.

"I told y'all this was going to happen, but did y'all listen to me? No! I hope that pussy is worth it. 'Cause when our parents find out that y'all let a wet cunt distract you from what we were raised for, they will never hand over their seats. I'll be stuck living under my dad's rules until he deems me ready for leadership." Holder heaves out a sigh of defeat. I didn't know he was under so much pressure. Shit, am I giving too much power to my past and it's defining all these men's futures too?

"First off, it's not her fault her crazy ex is doing all this. And secondly, fuck off Holder. You don't get to talk to her that way, ever. Besides, we can handle it now that we know what is going on. You're not alone in this. Our parents don't even have to know shit is going on if we keep this between us. We'll have to take the snitch out to the cabin until we can clean the mess up though. We'll move him tonight." Cole says, taking up the responsibility of fixing what I've now laid in their laps.

I refuse to let them deal with my problem. Now that I'm home, and have Old Man's backing, I don't need anyone to clean this mess up for me. When I'm done with the scummy dipshit, also known as my ex, there won't be enough of him left to clean up. I can't get my rant out of my mouth before the guys are all nodding and agreeing on their own plan. Men... I can't help but see the apprehension in Holder's eyes. Mr. "sex-on-a-stick" has some secrets that even his brothers don't know.

"Demon are you ready for your surprise? We're all here now anyway." Fletcher says, a smile spreading across half of his face till the point it's almost creepy.

"I'm gonna be heading out. Y'all have fun," comes from Holder's back as he walks towards the bedroom door.

"Wait a minute, Hold. You're going to want to see this. Ayida, sweets, go get some clothes on so Holder here can actually keep his eyes in his head." Fletcher is getting some kind of kick from this. I don't know what they have planned, but I'm starting to get worried.

"Fine. But first I want to clear the air. Since Y'all are going to keep pestering and aggravating me. It's not that I dislike Ayida, even though she was a major bitch the day we met-"

"Oh, hell no! You were an asshole that day. You started in pickin' on me and I was already having a shitty day. What did you think was going to happen? I was going to giggle and kiss your ass because you're hot? Nope, not that kind of girl!" Holder is slack jawed.

"She really isn't that kind of girl. On 'Its' bad days we give it bacon and coffee as soon as It pops Its head out of hell. Then a constant source of chocolate and or bacon is required to keep the reaping at bay." What the actual fuck? They honestly act like I'm Satan himself.

"Y'all are all weird as fuck, but I digress. I didn't mean to start off our day like that. I was going to befriend you to get closer with Old Man, but I stuck my foot in my mouth. Anyway, even if it pains me to say this... I'm sorry for what has gone down between us. I'm not looking to fuck you like these idiots. I still think it's a terrible idea, but I also don't want to push my brothers away. They are the only real family I have left. I would do anything for them. So, making up with you isn't the worst thing they could ask for," he finishes, reaching his hand out in my direction.

My brain misfires as I'm reaching out for his

hand and I jerk it back to my body like it about to be gnawed off. "Ummm no. You're gonna have to do better after everything you just said about my wet cunt. Remember? Now I'm all for making up and being friends, but a simple sorry won't cut it. I even understand you are under lots of pressure with everything going on, but I didn't deserve those nasty comments and neither did they." Gesturing to the guys as they nod along.

"Dude, that was some douchebag stuff. She deserves better." Cole chimes in.

"Okay, okay. Y'all are right. So, what's it gonna be? What do I have to do to get in the Princess' good graces? Beg and plead? Do your laundry? Just let me have it." Holder says while running his hands through his golden hair. He might be a douche canoe, but he is one fine ass douche canoe.

"Princess? Maybe the Princess of Hell," Fletcher teases.

"Fletcher, you're a dick. Wasn't you going to show me something?" I say with a voice so sweet it might have given me cavities.

"Yes! Yes, I did! Let's go see your surprise, Princess!" Squeezing me in a tight side hug and tugging me up from the bed.

"Wait! My clothes!" Too late. My death grip kept the sheet in place in front of me, but my bare rear end was poking out for all to see. Gathering the sheet in a toga style and blushing wildly, I dart off to the closet before I can hear anything the guys have to say. You never know what's going to come out of their deviant mouths where my ass is concerned.

I don't return until my face is back to its normal ivory hue and not resembling a tomato. In my most comfy black leggings, and one of Clint's worn-in button ups, I make my way downstairs where all the commotion is coming from.

"What the fuck is that thing? Have y'all lost y'all's minds? She is going to hate it! That thing is too scary even for me." Oh no what the hell have they gone and done now.

"Who the fuck are you? Get the fuck out my house!" Comes a screeching garbled voice. They want to talk about me being a demon, but whatever that was sounds like it just crawled straight out the bowels of Hell to reap the souls of the Sons of Fortune.

Swinging the French doors leading into the game room open, I find all four guys gathered around the pool table. All of them jerk to attention at my arrival. Interesting...

"What y'all got there? Did y'all get me my own demon?" I ask, sashaying in their direction.

"Okay Blue. Don't freak out. This is probably not what you were expecting or even wanting, but we're trying to do a good deed. So please just give it a chance. If you don't like it, we'll figure out something else." Clint is the most nervous I've ever seen him.

"Y'all are acting like y'all bought me a bomb for

a present. It's starting to scare me a little."

Pushing through the muscled bodies surrounding the table I finally see my prize. "OMG! Who is this gorgeous creature? What's your name cutie pie? You guys! Y'all didn't have to do this but thank you! He is perfect! Is it a he? I don't want to offend it!" I squeal while leaning down to get a better look at my new best friend *whether it likes it or not*.

This bird is barely a bird. The few feathers he has are a muted gray color. His cute beady eyes are wide with interest looking back at me. He has bald spots covering seventy-five percent of his body, so you can see his soft wrinkled skin easily. With a slight twitch he does a skip hop movement towards me and I feel like my heart might burst. He is adorable! *He will be the best sidekick ever!*

"You can't be serious. That thing is seriously ugly. Like scary ugly." Giving Cole a scathing glare, I hold my arm out towards the unique animal. His head turns and eyes study me intently before jumping to perch on my arm and ruffle his few feathers. Could he be any more perfect?

"What is this handsome fella's name? Yes, you are a pretty boy!" I coo to the twitchy flightless bird.

"This is Donut. He is supposed to be your alert bird, but so far, he just screams 'fuck you' all the time. He's a real asshole." Fletcher grumbles. Jealous man.

"Aww he just needs attention. Ain't that right,

Donut? Come on. I'm going to show you around. Yes, he's a pretty boy!" I can't help but talk to him like a child.

His wings shoot out and give a little shimmy before squawking, "Pretty boy! Donut- pretty boy!" Squealing in delight, I take the stairs two at a time.

"Yes, you are! I'm Ayida. Can you say Ayida? Thanks, you guys! This is the best day ever!"

"Assholes. Get the fuck out- assholes!"

This bird is definitely my soul mate!

Chapter Twenty: Fletcher

How the hell did this happen? That bird was supposed to supply me with days of laughter, aggravating Blue, before it ended up finding another home. Instead she loves the damn thing. She is already browsing bird clothes on my laptop while the featherless menace hops around the bed.

"Can you believe this shit? This was supposed to be hilarious. How did this turn so horribly wrong?" I know I'm pouting, and I don't care.

"You really should have seen it coming. She isn't like other people. She likes the different and deformed. She is with you after all." Cole thinks he's a fucking comedian again today.

"Ha. You're hilarious. I'm serious Cole. What are we going to do with that little asshole hopping around screaming cuss words at us all the time? Have you ever thought what sex is going to be like now? Life is just a barren wasteland now. It has no meaning when you have to share it with the likes of Donut." I grumble while laying my head in my hands.

"Talk about dramatic! It'll be okay. He has a

cage to stay in. Remember?" Clint yells from the kitchen. Making the Blue Demon her daily offering again.

"I don't know why she needs it today since she apparently received the best gift ever," I whine "Oh well, the Demon Princess gets what she wants and we keep our ears and nuts in place for another day." I joke, but she really is the sweetest most beautiful woman I've ever met. Every time I see her face light up laughing, I know I'm one lucky man. I would do anything to keep her smiling.

This girl gives her all in everything. There is nothing half assed or mediocre about her. She makes me feel loved, wanted, appreciated... I want to drown in the ocean that is Blue. She doesn't realize it, but she makes these days dealing with unbelievably bad people worth it. I know that after a long hard day is over, I'll get to see her. Smell her. Taste her. It's what keeps me going. I don't know how I lived this life before Ayida Underhill.

"Speaking of a cage... Holder I have your assignment to make everything up to me. I'm fixin' to go help Old Man clean up, and he has a doctor's appointment that I have to drive him to. Can you go get Donut a bigger cage, some toys, new feed and whatever else that will make him happy? Also keep him company while I'm gone, please and thank you. It must be scary being in a new place. Isn't it buddy?"

This woman is certifiably nuts. She acts like that

bird is a puppy. "Nope! Sorry, but hell to the no! I don't want to spend time with it. I don't even want to be in the same room as it. Anything else but this!" Holder thinks he is getting out of this, but we all know the truth. Blue gets what Blue wants.

"Sorry Hold, but this is your make-up mission. You've been a real twat waffle recently. Do this for me and I'll call it even." Sighing, Holder stands up from the table and steps in front of Blue.

"Deal. From now on we're friends and I'll take care of "Donut the Menace." My sweet Demon claps her hands and bounces on her toes before grabbing Holder in a bear hug.

His eyes shoot open wide as it registers what she is doing. He likes her more than a friend and he has a bad case of denial. Poor guy. He'll figure it out soon enough. He can't keep getting hugs from her without figuring out how he truly feels. The heart wants what the heart wants.

"Thank you! I'm gonna go get ready. Donut is going to be in his cage. I emailed you a list of what he needs. He is going to be so excited! Thank you again!" She says before flouncing back up the stairs.

"Damn that woman. Damn that stupid bird. I can't believe I have to go shopping for that goblin!" Yep, he has it bad for her. "I guess I'll see y'all asswipes later. Try not to get anymore demonic animals while I'm gone." He says shaking his head and leaves to go run his errands.

Stomping down the stairs is definitely a way to

get everyone's attention. Blue is not one to be ignored anyway. She makes her way into the dining room just as Clint brings out breakfast and a thermos of coffee. She has really been good for him. She is the human version to him as Donut is to her. He takes care of her and spoils her. Cole is almost as bad. Standing in front of me, stuffing bacon in her mouth, I can see how easy it would be to get wrapped around her little finger.

"Thank you for breakfast," she says while winking at Clint. "I think we need to have a conversation sometime soon about all that was said earlier this morning. I know we started this off as 'friends with benefits. Apparently, some things are changing. I just want to clear the air. I don't like things muddled."

Oh shit. I should have seen this coming. I don't really want to talk about feelings with the other guys. "I agree, but let's talk about that after tonight is handled." Thank you, Clint, - taking one for the team!

"Okay. I'll see you when I get back. Wish me luck. Old Man gets ornery at the doctors." Making her way to kiss Clint then myself. She tries to make it quick, but I wrap my arms around, pulling her into my lap. She smells like bacon, coffee, and sunshine. Delicious. I take my time smelling and nibbling her neck. Moaning and squirming on my lap is causing my cock to tent in my pants. Thankfully, she kisses me one more time before pushing herself up to standing and straightens her shirt. "I'll see y'all when I get back. Don't move the snitch before I get back. I want to be there." Not a good idea.

"Look Blue... You already have night terrors and PTSD. I don't know if this is a situation you need to be involved in." Clint jumps in before I can stop him.

"I know what I want and what I can handle. Please don't patronize me with your, 'she's too sensitive', ideas. Before I met y'all, Old Man had someone teach me basic self-defense and some weapons training. I might not be some 'big Billy badass' like y'all, but I can hold my own and I'll be fine. Now, y'all have a good day. Buh-bye!"

Well she settled that real quick. Now I'm curious what all she has learned. I see a challenge in my future.

Chapter Twenty-One: Ayida

Stupid men and their stupid "big dick energy" ideas. If they only knew everything I went through and all I've learned. When you've been locked in a dark closet with no food or drink only to have the shit beat out of you when the door finally opened... You see the world a little differently. So, when I moved back in with Old Man, he made sure I got the extensive training I needed. Not only to protect myself from the ex dick-weed, but to also prove to the rest of the Family I was as capable as the other heirs. I can handle anything I need to.

Pulling up to Old Man's house feels strange after being at Clint's so much. He is sitting on the porch smoking his menthol and drinking his coffee. I'm sure he has some shortbread cookies hidden somewhere nearby. It's one of his weaknesses. He loves sweets.

"How ya doing, Schatzi? Clint keeping you busy. ya know he's supposed to be working too. His momma and daddy ain't gonna be very happy to find out he's been shucking his duties to keep you entertained." Old Man loves to give me a hard time any way he can. He isn't actually mad; he just wants someone to fuck with.

"I hear ya Old Man. He is doing his work fine. He is just a glorified accountant after all."

My dad's RV business launders the Family's money. I tease, but Clint is responsible for moving the money either into offshore accounts or into stocks and bonds. He is actually incredibly good at what he does. He knows all there is about investing and hiding money.

"Yeah, yeah. You ready to get this show on the road? I've been waiting on you forever." I'm actually ten minutes early, but I'm not going to correct him. He doesn't like that at all.

"Yeah, come on." I turn the station to the country oldies station just for him. Hank Williams comes crooning with his guitar through the speakers right as Old Man fumbles his way into my two-door hatchback. It might not be pretty, but it got me out of the hell hole I was living in; it's the best damn car on the planet as far as I'm concerned. "I love this one. They just don't make 'em like this anymore."

Humming along with the catchy ditty old song, I can't help but gaze fondly at Old Man. My dad may be old and mean, but he's mine. He could have done a lot of things different or better, but I'm blessed just to have someone that helps the way he does.

Driving thirty minutes to his neurologist, it's mostly silence in the car except for him singing along occasionally.

"We're here. You want me to wait in the car or you okay with me in the room?" Old Man is big on privacy.

"You can come in if you can keep your thoughts to yourself." Already pissy- fun times.

"I can do that. Let's hurry up though. I still have to run your errands and get back to Clint's. We have business tonight." My cheeks burn at the startling realization of what just came out of my mouth.

"Is that what the kids call it these days? Back in my day it was called fuckin'." He is bent over holding his knees. Laughing at my expense.

"I figured back in your day mitosis was still the

norm. Ya know back in the Paleozoic era?" Yep I just dropped some high school knowledge on him.

"Are you trying to say I'm older than the dinosaurs? That was a nerdy comeback. You sure you're not hanging out with Cole?" I haven't told Dad what was going on. He just came to the conclusion I was seeing Clint and I didn't correct him. I mean technically he is right.

"Well, Old Man, I've been meaning to talk to you about that." Waiting for him to sign-in, I gather my thoughts. I need to tell him. It's going to start getting around if the guys are serious about me being more than "friends with benefits". The last thing I want is Dad hearing it from someone else and him catching any flak from the Family. He would go off on them, but that's not the point.

Sitting down, I turn towards my dad and look him in the eye. He doesn't like bullshitters either, so I reconcile my spiraling thoughts and try to be as diplomatic about this as possible... "I'm not dating just Clint. I am, in fact, dating Clint, Cole, and Fletcher. I know you won't approve, but I figured I needed to tell you sooner rather than later. I don't want any negativity about it, please. Just living my-"

His big, wrinkled, bruised hand covers mine. I didn't realize I was rubbing a hole in my jeans. "Schatzi, nothing you could do would make me think any less of you. I'm so proud of the woman you have become. Lord knows it wasn't my doing. You have grown so much in the last few months. I'll support you no matter what. Even one of those boys is worth ten times what your shit head ex was. So, I would say you're doing rather good. I'm gonna give them hell though. That's just your Old Man's way."

Tears pouring down my face and hiccupping breaths is not the way I wanted the nurse to see me when she called him back to the room.

After cleaning my face up, I turn to Old Man and wrap my arms around him. I feel genuine relief. He could have reacted in a hundred different ways, but he chose love. The one thing I have been looking for since my mom died. He gave it freely. I don't know if I've ever felt more peaceful than I do now.

"Now don't start the fluffy stuff, Schatzi." Old

Man harrumphed. "I'm just telling ya the truth. Your momma would have been proud too. Just remember that." His squeeze makes my heart swell with his declaration of acceptance.

A knock on the door breaks up our hug fest. "Mr. Underhill. How are we doing today?" A middle-aged man with chestnut hair and thin wire framed glasses walks in with a laptop in his hands. "This must be that daughter you were talking about. Ayida, isn't it?" He says while sticking his hand out to greet me.

"Yes, I am. I'm glad to know Frank has been talking about me." I sneak a look at Old Man. His cheeks sure look rosy.

"Only good things. He was sure happy to have

you back around. Now down to business. We have the results back." Looking back and forth between the doctor and Old Man, I'm confused.

"What results? I thought this was just a follow-up." Old Man gives me a look I can't quite place.

"Before you got back, I was having some issues. I was forgetting things and having problems with my emotions. So, Doc here ran some tests." He answers on a sigh, looking already droopy with exhaustion.

I don't know how to feel about that. I wish he would have said something earlier... I can't help thinking this is somehow ominous.

"So, back to the results. Sadly, it does look like early onset Alzheimer's. The good news is medicine can most likely delay any progression for a while.

Sometimes the meds don't work, or you can have a reaction. If that happens, we'll deal with it. Just know this is not the end. We plan on doing everything we can to keep you where you are now." The Doc looking melancholy as he breaks down the news.

That's a damn good thing the Doc is up for a challenge because I know Old Man and he won't let it get to a bad point. He has too much pride and dignity for that. "Do y'all have any questions for me?" The doctor gives us a sympathetic glance.

"I think I need to wrap my brain around this information before I can ask anything else, but thanks Doc." Old Man says, reaching out to shake the doctor's hand.

"I'll send in your prescription and we'll do a follow-up in two weeks to make sure it's agreeing with you. It was nice to meet you, Ayida. Wish it were under better circumstances." Nodding my head in agreement I shake his hand. I still feel in a daze. Like all this isn't real. I know that Old Man isn't dying anytime soon, but I can't help but feel dread.

"Come on Schatzi, let's get going. Got places to go, people to fuck with." Dragging me out of my inner turmoil.

"Sure, thing Old Man. Want to grab lunch first?" Old Man loves to eat.

"I could eat. See ya later Doc." I wrap my arm through his as we walk back to my clunker.

"You want to talk about this, or just let it

simmer?" One heart to heart might be enough for Old Man for the day. I still have to have another deep conversation with the guys and my emotional wellbeing is already on the line.

"Schatzi, let that shit simmer like gumbo." We are more alike than I thought.

"Speaking of gumbo, where ya want to go eat?" Like I need to ask.

"Judy's has lunch."

..."Of course."

Chapter Twenty-Two: Cole

Oh shit! "Don't look now, but here comes Blue and Old Man." Warning Clint before he gets blindsided.

"Fuckkk, what do we do?" Clint grimaces. What does he mean asking me like I know what to do?

"Act normal, I guess. I don't know, just keep eating. Head down. No direct eye contact. He can smell fear..." Fingers crossed they don't even notice us.

"Clint? Cole? What are y'all doing here? I thought y'all was busy today? Did y'all check in on Donut before y'all left? I hope my little angel is okay." That girl can ramble with the best of them.

"What the hell is Donut and what are y'all doing here and not at the lot? Cole?" Old Man's stern eyes landing on me. Fuck Clint and his need to eat at Judy's.

"Well sir, we were working, but Clint's stomach was growling so loud, he was being disruptive, and Judy's is his favorite place to eat- so here we are. Oh, and Donut is the pet bird we got Ayida. It's a poor psychotic creature that crawled out of hell and burned most of his feathers off on the trip up." I say in one breath.

Old Man does not look impressed. So, I almost shit my pants when he bursts out laughing. "Y'all tried to use a bird to get in my daughter's pants? Well that's a first. But for real, who's idea was it to share my daughter like she was a Netflix password?" I'm impressed he knows about Netflix but scared as hell that he knows we share Blue.

"Sir, it's not like that. We all care about Blue. She means a lot to us." That's the understatement of the year. I'm falling in love with her. Her spunky attitude, her sense of humor, and her dark side. She is everything I didn't know I needed and more. I just hope she feels the same. I want to talk to her about everything, but I know how she is when she gets emotional.

"Blue is a surprisingly good nickname for my Schatzi. Not just because of her hair either. It's because she is a blue person. Deep like the ocean, but bright like the sky. That's my girl. Y'all hurt her or make her cry, I'll skin y'all, douse y'all in gasoline, set ya on fire and hang ya in my house by the balls for her to beat the shit out ya at her leisure before I feed ya to the gators. Understand me?" If his expression is any evidence, he ain't joking. I know I heard Clint audibly gulp. He hasn't said a word or looked in Old Man's direction this whole time. Smart guy.

"Understood, sir. Now y'all have a nice day. Me and Clint here have work to do. Bye Mr. Underhill. Bye Blue." Giving him a quick handshake and her a peck on the forehead, I make a beeline for the door and don't wait to see if Clint is following.

Back in the safety of my car, I see Clint coming out looking a little pale. I wish I felt bad, but he didn't open his mouth to help me.

"What the fuck, dude? You were out of there faster than a goose with a rocket strapped to its ass. Why the hell did you leave me with them?" I don't even know what that means, but I get the gist of it.

"Well, where was you when I was in the hot seat?" His head bowed in shame.

"I didn't know what to do. I panicked, okay? I

didn't know if she had told him or not and then he just blurted it out. I could feel my heart beating in my ears. I'm still freaking out. I'm sorry, dude." I know he is.

Clint really is a good guy. His job is the nicest and most on the up and up out of all of ours. He is more white color. I'm somewhere in between. I handle the dealers and buyers for black market guns, ammo, and some drugs that the heads feel isn't a big threat. Weed mostly. After everything is sold, I use the money to buy RVs and then turn around and sell them. The Family ends up with clean money to do even more deals. It doesn't hurt to have access to an unlimited supply of guns, too. I might be ridin' nerdy, but I also don't mind ridin' dirty. I love going to Clint's and trying out all the new toys I get. The guys don't mind either. It usually becomes a competition. Clint and I have the best aim. Mine from starting early training with my dad and uncle. Clint gets his from the Navy.

Holder doesn't think we know, but it's easy to see, he likes the up close and personal method when it comes to interrogations and killing'. That man doesn't smile much, but after getting his hands bloody he'll be grinning for hours. We don't care. It pays to have someone with bloodlust in a Family like ours.

Fletcher, now he would rather not fight, but if he has to it's just like the rest of his personality- wild. He fights like a drunk college kid. Not in a bad way. He just gives no fucks and goes in swinging, balls to the wall. He will always be a live wire.

"Drop me at the lot. I have some paperwork and transfers to do for Old Man and I don't like dealing with Jimmy. I just have bad vibes from him. Not the smuggler kind, but the 'sell my grandma for a pizza', kind." Jimmy is a worm, but a necessary worm. He is my contact bringing guns and drugs from the border.

"Fine, just be ready to go when I get back. I can't wait to see Holder." I chuckle as I pull into the parking lot of the RV dealership.

"I know! How much do you want to bet that bird has driven him nuts? Blue was a genius to give him that punishment." She is a conniving, evil genius.

"I'll be surprised if that bird is still alive when we

get back. I would feel sorry for Blue, but that would

fix one gremlin problem."

One can dream.

Chapter Twenty-Three: Fletcher

I'm so excited! I've waited all day for this moment. Quietly opening the front door to Clint's house, I try to sneak in.

Only to have a screeching, "Fucking- Fletcher! Asshat- Fletcher!" meet my ears.

"How the hell does that goblin know my name? And how did he know I was here? I was quiet!" Holder's snickering ass waltzes through the kitchen door holding a beer in one hand and that damn bird perched on his shoulder.

"Don't you know birds have excellent hearing? I decided to spend my time today learning about Donut since I was having to deal with the little fucker. Turns out African grey parrots are extremely smart and have many talents. They also can become extremely attached to multiple people and I have decided my way into Blue's good graces is to make this bird my new best friend." He smirks in my direction after taking a sip of his beer.

"You clever motherfucker. I wish I would have

thought of that. That still doesn't explain how he knows my name." I say walking to the refrigerator and retrieving my own beer.

"Well, isn't it obvious? I showed Donut all of our pictures and taught him some fun nicknames." He is beaming. Prideful bastard.

"Well fuck you and that bird. Is Blue back yet?" I ask as I notice Donut nuzzling up against Holder's chest and face. He really did buddy up with the partially feathered freak.

"She called earlier; said she was on her way. I need to talk to y'all about tonight." He says nervously. I can't help but see his twitchy movements.

Before I can ask anything the door slams open

and I hear Blue hollering at Cole. "My Donut is alive! I talked to Holder earlier and he was taking good care of him. You and Fletch are the only ones that want him gone, everybody else likes him." She says stomping into the kitchen to see us standing there. "There's my baby! Come here pretty boy. How was your day with Holder?" She coos to the beady eyed bird.

"Holder's boy. Holder's boy." What the actual hell is going on? "Asshat- Fletcher." I'm so fucking done! This bird and Holder are dead.

"Aww did my baby learn something new today. Holder did spend time with you, didn't he?" Rubbing his mostly bare head as he ruffles the few feathers he has and bobs his head.

"Okay enough talking about and to the bird. Holder has something he needs to tell us about tonight." Might as well get to the point.

"I was just gonna talk with the guys. Blue, you can go check out Donut's new digs if you want." Uh-oh I can already see where this is headed.

"Excuse me, Holder, but I will be part of this. Me and the other guys have already had this discussion today. So, please let's get this going." Holder looks like he might choke on his words.

"Well... ya see... when the little asshole that my men caught told me why he was there. I may have... okay I did overreact." Ahh fuck.

"What did you do, Hold?" Like Clint really needs to ask. We all know. Well Ayida probably doesn't, but she'll find out soon enough. That's just Holder. He would never hurt an innocent person, but he can get carried away in his questioning. We know he has some bloody tendencies, but we love him anyway.

"I got worried and then I got mad. I'm sorry. Can we please not make a big deal out of this? We can catch another guy tonight or later this week and question them." Blue, to my surprise, doesn't look phased. She reaches out briefly and squeezes his hand.

"Hold, it's okay. I've accepted you, all y'all, without reservations. I know what it feels like when you lose control when you embrace the darkness. That's what happened the night I beat my ex. I would have killed him, but I pulled back. Now I wish

I wouldn't have used so much restraint. I mean, what would you do for the ones you love? Personally, I would bleed every enemy dry with a smile on my face." She finishes with a somewhat manic smile, glancing at all our faces, waiting for a reply. Maybe our Blue is more like Holder than we thought.

"Okay let's just move along. The next issue, we need a plan of action." Clint the ever-ready soldier.

"I was thinking we could wait around tonight and see if anyone shows up. I'll stand guard like I have been doing and y'all can hide inside. If anyone shows, we grab them and take them to the cabin." Holder blurts. Not a horrible plan.

"Okay and then what do we do? Are we going

to bring this up to the heads or just try and deal with it without them finding out?" I don't like going behind their backs. They have ways of knowing everything.

"Let's see how tonight goes and go from there." Clint says rubbing his hands through his hair.

"Okay then- good talk! I'm going to check out Donut's new space. Y'all let me know when y'all are ready. Come on, baby. Come show me what Holder got for you." Ayida says taking Donut and climbing the stairs to what has basically become "our room".

"Wait a minute! We are supposed to be having a more important conversation! Remember?" Clint hollers up the stairs.

"Well, come on up if you want to." Brat.

"Well... should we?" Cole's back to his bashful self.

"Before we go up there, we need to be on the same page. I love her. I know I do. So... are y'all in love with her? Are we going to keep this situation going? I'm good with how it is. I just want her to know the truth. That, for me, this isn't just 'friends with benefits' anymore." Clint says, laying everything out in the open.

"I feel the same. She is one of a kind, and I would be stupid to give her up just because y'all love her too." Cole says with red cheeks.

That just leaves me. I fancy myself good with emotions, but that doesn't mean I like talking about them with the guys. "Oh, hell! Yes, I love her. Yes, I want to be with her, and I don't care if she loves all of us, but have y'all wondered if maybe she doesn't want this or maybe she only likes one or two of us? What then?" It's called being emotionally vulnerable, and I'm not very fond of it when I'm with my brothers.

"Then we deal with that when it comes. Just like everything else in life. I can't keep going like this and not tell her how I feel." Clint says, ending the conversation and jogging up the stairs.

"Y'all coming or nah?" He yells down to us.

"Well, this has been sweet and everything, but I'm gonna go set up for tonight. Have a great rest of the afternoon, and I'll see y'all later." Holder says, making his way to the front door and waving over his shoulder.

"Well, no better time than the present. Let's do this, brother." Clapping Cole on the shoulder and leading him up the stairs.

Time to tell our lady how we feel.

Chapter Twenty-Four: Ayida

"Sweet boy! Look at your new cage! Holder went above and beyond. No wonder you like him." Petting Donut's beak and chest, I admire Holder's handiwork. He really must want to make up for everything. He got everything I asked for and more. He put everything together and hung my baby a treat bar up too. He did a really good job. I'll have to tell him later.

Hearing feet coming down the hallway, I sit Donut on his new perch to enjoy his snack. "Here we go, baby. Let's hope everything goes like we want." I take a deep breath right as Clint comes barreling through the door.

"Blue, ya gonna make me chase you down just to have a simple chat? Keep that up and I'm going to swat that sweet ass of yours." My pussy spasms just hearing his words.

"I guess I'll just have to see if you mean it." Stalking towards me like a wolf, I can feel his predatory presence surrounding me. I wonder if this is how a deer feels right before teeth meet flesh. I'm not about to wait around to see what happens. I squeal and bolt to the left just barely missing his outstretched fingers.

I can hear Donut screeching behind me, "Damn you- Clint! Damn you!"

I sprint for the stairs as fast as I can, but I already sense Clint coming up behind me. "Can't run from me, Baby Blue."

Watch and see.

I'm two feet from the stairs when Fletcher and Cole's heads come into view. "Grab her!" Clint yells from behind me.

I dart to the right and book it to the first open door I see. It just so happens to be the guys' gym room. I turn, shutting and locking the door as fast as my hands will go.

"Blue… we know you're in there. You can't hide." Clint says as he jiggles the door handle.

"I may not be able to hide, but I sure can fight. Y'all didn't think I could handle tonight. If y'all can get in here, I'll show you what I can handle." I love taunting them. I've learned the last couple of weeks, if you make them work for it, they fuck twice as hard.

"Baby Blue, we are legit criminals. Raised as such and you honestly think we can't get through this door?" I can't help but giggle.

"Of course, I know y'all can get through, silly. I'm just trying to aggravate you."

I can hardly breathe when I hear Fletcher say, "You little wench. You wait till I get my hands on you. I'm going to fuck the sass right out of you."

This is going to be fun. I hear the clicking of the lock and ready myself. Pulling my fists to my face, blocking the way I was taught, and planting my feet. I'm about to rock their fucking socks off.

Swinging the door open, Clint rushes me. I deliver a teasing pop to his cheek while sidestepping his efforts to grab me.

"Gotta be quicker than that." I tease with another pop to his ribs. Before I get another swing in, I'm grabbed around the waist from behind.

"You have to stay aware of your surroundings, Blue." Cole's whisper in my ear makes me shiver.

The chase isn't over yet though.

"You need to stop underestimating me." I murmur before thrusting my head back to make contact with his cheekbone. His grip loosens enough that I can send an elbow to his ribs and twist out of his arms.

It only takes a second before Fletcher is standing right in front of me. He reaches out and grabs my arm and pulls me flush with his chest. "Blue, I'm not playing this game with you. Don't move." He breathes his words into my ear. I feel another hot, hard body pressed to my back.

"You better listen, Princess. Fletch has been waiting to spank that juicy ass just as much as I have." My pussy is betraying me. I feel the wetness on my thighs the same time I feel fingers sliding up to meet it. Cole is kneeling next to us running his hands up my legs. Squeezing and kneading the sensitive flesh. Fingers push the edge of my shirt up and over my breasts.

"Are you going to behave if I let you go?" Fletcher murmurs while licking the crest of my ear. Goosebumps break out all over my body.

"Mmmhmm," I whimper as Cole undresses my lower half and Clint plucks at my already hardened nipples.

"Blue, look at me." Fletcher commands as he runs his hand up my neck, clasping my face and pulling me an inch from his. "Do you think you are ready for some extra fun this time?" Running his thumb over my bottom lip before kissing me hard enough to bruise. Fingers brush my core just enough to send tremors down my legs. Clint pinching and rolling my barred nipples while kneading my breasts. The combined sensations have my legs turning to jelly.

"Yes. Please. I'm ready for all of it." I'm practically begging, but I'm so turned on and needy I can't stop myself.

Taking their time undressing, I memorize every dip and curve of muscle. Every scar and mark. Every dimple, every tattoo, every quirk of a smile and grin. They are fierce, but beautiful and I'm in awe of the feelings they cause to stir in my chest.

Scooping me up, Clint moves to the weight

bench before sitting down with me in his lap. The feeling of his warm skin causing mine to tingle. Grabbing my thighs and pulling them apart, he slides his finger over my sensitive nub. My back arches as I let my head drop onto his shoulder. I want more stimulation, but he just lifts his finger to his mouth and tastes the wetness left there.

"She tastes so damn good. Fletcher, you want a taste?" He asks while spreading my lips with his fingers. Showing Fletcher every inch of me.

"How can I say no when she looks so deliciously pink?" He answers while kneeling in front of me. It takes every ounce of control I have not to grind myself on his face when his tongue slides in and out of my folds. His tongue then stiffening as he proceeds to tongue fuck my core deeply before circling back and flicking out and over my clit.

"Mmm. You are right. She tastes amazing." He dives back down and starts lapping at my already sensitive cunt.

I feel myself growing closer to the climax I crave. When his finger dips into my entrance just long enough to get wet I almost cry out in frustration, but then I feel it somewhere that's never been touched. It's an odd, but not unwelcoming sensation.

Fletch swirls his tongue over my clit while his slick finger starts to put pressure on my tightest hole with just the tip. Wriggling and moaning, I can feel his tongue pushing my orgasm out of my body. Just as I'm about to explode in his mouth, he slides his finger past the ring of muscle as he sucks my clit in his mouth at the same time. He obviously has experience in this area and I'm happy to be on the receiving end of his expertise. It feels so good, really good. It's making mumbling, stuttering, unhuman noises escape my mouth as my whole-body flexes as an orgasm rocks through me.

It isn't until I feel Clint rolling me over onto his chest that I come back down from the high I'm riding. "Baby Blue that must have been a good one. I think you were speaking in tongues." Clint's mischievous eyes meet mine. Kissing the corner of my mouth and down my neck, I can already feel my body ready for round two.

The smooth tip of Clint's cock lining up with my soaking wet slit. "Fletcher must have done something new. Your pussy is dripping. What did he do, Blue? Was it him rubbing your tight little asshole that pushed you over the edge? Do you want him to push his cock into you while I bury mine in your tight wet cunt?" His words have me grinding on him. Wiggling back to try and get the relief I crave.

Two strong rough hands land on my hips. "Blue, if you want this to feel good, you need to relax and be still. Let us do the work." Fletcher says in a low growl while rubbing his member around my pussy lips, dipping inside to coat his fat cock head in my cum. I glance back over my shoulder and see Cole watching and rubbing his hard as steel monster cock.

"I'll be over there as soon as they get you situated to put something big in that dirty mouth of yours." He grins at me. Clint pulls my face back to his and licks the seams of my lips. Tasting my moans as Fletcher slides his cock between my ass cheeks. Adding more pressure with every moan I make. His tip finally pushes through and a sharp sting follows.

I go to cry out only to have Clint kiss me roughly. Sucking down the silent cry. "Shhh Baby Blue. If you relax it will be better very soon." Clint whispers into my lips as he runs his hands down my spine. Bumping his hips up to mine, the head of his cock brushes my clit sending tingles into my belly.

My moan is swallowed as his tongue wars with mine; teeth and lips trying to claim one another.

Fletcher barely moves. Giving me time to adjust. It still stings, but I can feel myself starting to relax around his cock. Wiggling around, I test the feeling and it feels good. "More. I can take more." I moan as I look back over my shoulder at Fletch.

"Damn Blue. You are so fucking hot and tight. It's almost impossible not to pound into you right now." Pushing in an inch only to pull out, he works his cock into me at a pace that's driving me mad. Over half of his cock is buried in my ass when I finally feel Clint's hips thrust upwards pushing against my pussy lips with his stiff member.

"You ready for the second one, Blue?" Cole smirks as he runs his fingers into my hair. Pulling my lips to his, he nibbles and sucks on them, his beard slightly tickling me, before Clint pushes his long hard cock past my folds and drives straight into my core in one hard thrust.

Cole holds my mouth to his while I struggle with the feeling of being stretched to the limits between Clint and Fletcher. I don't even get comfortable when Fletcher pushes into the hilt. I'm going to be sore tomorrow, but right now in this moment, I'm in pure bliss.

The room is now starting to smell like sex and its intoxicating; a wonderful feeling of pain and pleasure is quickly leading me towards another orgasm. Two large cocks stretching my walls thin. When they start moving in time with each other, Clint slips his hand between us to rub my clit with his thumb, and I feel like my soul has left my body. Pushing and pulling, each one hits a spot deep inside me that makes my stomach flip.

"You need something to keep that pretty mouth busy? I think choking on my cock is just what you need." Cole growls into my ear right before grabbing a handful of my blue hair and turning my head toward his waiting magic-stick.

Taking his thumb and pulling my mouth wide open, he pushes his throbbing cock head in and begins to fuck my mouth. Wrapping his tattooed hand around my long hair he uses it as leverage to push me to the base and pull me back to the tip. One hand moves to my jaw so he can angle my head in a better way, and my saliva starts to drip down his shaft. He needn't have worried though, I am practically begging to gag on his cock.

"Blue, I love fucking your throat. That way I can see my brothers ravaging that beautiful pussy and virgin ass. Does it feel good to be split between two big cocks? Do you want to gush all over Clint's cock when Fletch cums all over that pretty ass?" His words are the catalyst that sends me over the edge. Fire shoots through my veins and my vision spins. I have never felt anything like this.

In the back of mind, I can hear Fletcher groaning my name almost like a benediction invoking divine help. Soon I feel his hot cum pool on my lower back, but I'm powerless to do or say anything. My orgasm is still racking my body. These men truly have me dicklashed.

"Blue, I have to cum. I can't wait any longer. Your pussy feels too damn good." Clint grinds out, grabbing my hip and jerking me down on his cock hard. I feel him swelling and throbbing inside of me. It sends another rush of pleasure through my body.

Moaning and humming in contentment around Cole's massive cock, I reach out and start tickling and massaging his balls with my fingernails. I look up and see the lust in his eyes. "Come for me Cole. I want your cum dripping from my lips and down my chin." I beg in a whispery whine.

"Mmmm… you're such a naughty girl. You ready? I want you to swallow my cum, Baby." Thrusting his cock to the back of my throat I can feel his seed shooting out of him. "That's my good girl. Take all that cum. I bet your pussy is a mess with all the cum Clint pumped into you." He finishes with a strained groan. A few more pumps into my mouth and he is drained and gently pulling out. I wantonly lick my lips of every last drop of him.

"Blue, you are the woman of my dreams. That was amazing. You are amazing." Cole says stroking my hair and face. Walking away to get a washcloth I can't help but look at his firm ass. I bet I could bounce a quarter off of it. Damn, I'm a thirsty bitch. I just got done getting fucked by these three men and I'm ready again. Truthfully though I don't think I could ever get tired of them in my bed or in my life.

Closing my eyes, I relax into Clint's embrace and

just enjoy the attention of him and Fletcher rubbing my hair and back. I don't even realize I'm dozing off until I feel Cole laying me in bed and climbing in behind me. "A quick nap before tonight's stakeout won't hurt. It's better for you to be rested before having to deal with all four of us." I am exhausted.

"Blue. We came up here to talk and YOU, little vixen, got us distracted." Clint says, lightly swatting my ass cheek. I can't help but giggle. "I don't know what you're talking about. You're the ones that chased me." Smiling at him as innocently as I knew how, his face goes serious.

"I'll always chase you. As long as you let me. I would chase you to the ends of the earth. Blue, your one of a kind. The girl I've been waiting for and I have to tell you even if you don't want to hear it. I am hopelessly in love with you." My heart is beating so fast it might just stop working all together.

"He's not the only one, Blue. We all feel the same way about you. You bring us closer together. You're the missing piece to a puzzle we didn't know was unfinished." Fletcher says from my feet with conviction. I'm flying. I didn't know falling in love would be possible after everything I've been through. I thought my heart was broken in a way that no one would ever understand. These men though, they just wiggled their way in without me even knowing it.

"Blue, you don't have to say anything. We just need you to know how we feel and that we're here for you." Cole says in my ear.

"I want to say something. I'm not the most eloquent person but... I fucking love you guys, too. I didn't want to. I never intended to get attached to someone again and here I am getting attached to y'all." I'm crying. Another thing that I always seem to be doing since the Sons of Fortune came into my life.

Wiping my tears, Clint presses his lips to mine in a tender kiss. Sharing his emotions with me. Cole's lips and tongue dance on my neck and ear. Tickling and massaging all while Fletcher kisses and nibbles the back of my knee and thigh. All the physical and emotional connections making me soar. Pure happiness and love fill my soul right before sleep overtakes me.

I've never slept so well.

Chapter Twenty-Five: Holder

Pulling back into Clint's driveway, I have a mixture of feelings in my gut. Happy to be back with my brothers, anxiety about being around Ayida, anger that my obsession caused us to have to do this tonight, and maybe a bit of sadness that I'm not in there kissing the Blue Demon too. It must be done though. I would feel even worse if something happened to Ayida. When did this wild, blue-haired, beautiful girl become such a bright star in my dark night?

I walk into the house and I'm assaulted by the smell of gumbo, as well as the screeching background noise of Donut the menace, "Holder's baby! Holder's baby!"

"Hold? I'm back here! I figured we could all eat together before we go. I don't want to be stuck somewhere all night without something in my belly. So, I made my Nana's famous gumbo." Ayida hollers from the kitchen.

"I see Donut is doing his job. He sure has picked up on everyone's names quickly." Walking to the dining room I find said flightless bird perched on one of his stands looking out at the window. I walk over and give him a quick scratch under the beak.

Moments later, Ayida comes flouncing through the swinging door with a giant pot in her hands. She looks even more alluring than earlier. Her hair pulled up into a high ponytail, makes her heart shaped face and feminine neck even more pronounced. Her feminine curves are so appealing, but her eyes are what will forever catch my attention. Drawing me in. She shows all her emotions through them. She doesn't hold anything back like I do. Her smile takes my breath away and I feel horrible making her upset in the beginning.

"Because he's the bestest bird in the whole

world. Yes, he is!" She coos at the bird while rubbing his head. She is so close and smells so good.

"He is definitely a special one." The little goblin has started to grow on me.

"Let's eat. The guys will be down any minute. I woke up before them to get a shower. So, they are just now catching up." She says with a smirk. I have a good idea why they needed showers. Now all I'm going to be able to think about is my best friends fucking the girl sitting next to me all night.

"It sure does smell good. Thanks for asking me to stay. I know we got off on the wrong foot. I was being an ass. I just don't do well with new people. I have my brothers and my kid sister, but I can't be the real me with them. I can't be the real me with anyone, but at least they put up with me. I wouldn't know what to do without them." I don't know why I'm telling her all this. Maybe because of how she acted when I admitted I fucked up and killed the whistle-blower. She wasn't scared. She didn't look at me differently. She was kind and understanding.

"I think you could show your brothers any side of you and they would accept and love you. They respect you; they trust you, they are loyal to you, and they really do care. As far as me? Don't worry about it. I've had a lot worse said about me. I have thick skin. Literally and figuratively."

How can she be so at ease with talking about what she went through? I guess everyone copes differently and this mafia princess is stronger than most. I dive into the steaming bowl of gumbo she pushes my way. It is heaven. Usually Clint is our cook if we eat together or we go out to Judy's. It's nice having a woman around just to hear a feminine voice and smell something pretty.

"This is so good. Your Nana taught you well." She just hums her thanks as she slurps away at her food. Even eating she is captivating. I have to get a grip on myself. She wouldn't want me after everything. She wouldn't want me if she knew how fucked up, I was in the bedroom. My brothers are the exact opposite of me. They like control and know how to take it without traumatizing someone. It's best if me and Blue just stay friends.

"I smell food!" Of course, Fletcher would be the

first one down to eat. "Hey Hold! You already eating without us?" He pouts while scooping up his bowl.

"Don't blame him. Y'all took too long. Now, y'all better hurry up and eat so we can get going," she insists firmly. I can't help but to get turned on when she gets bossy. I reach down under the table to nonchalantly readjust my dick that apparently likes her tone.

"Yes ma'am," I reply huskily back. It's only a few minutes before two more sets of feet come lumbering down the stairs.

"Smells good, Blue. We have dessert tonight, too?" Clint says grinning wickedly in her direction.

"Not if we don't hurry up and get done with everything. I'll be too sleepy and ready for bed."

Popping her hip out as she totes the almost empty pot back through the swinging door.

"So, Holder, you gonna stay for dessert tonight?" Fletcher teases.

"I don't think Ayida would care for that."

"Care for what? What are y'all planning?" Damn it! I will not get roped into this. Not right now.

"Nothing Blue. Just picking on Holder." Clint says with a smirk. They know exactly what they are doing.

"Well y'all better stop pickin' on him. Only I should be doing that. Right pretty boy?" What the hell?

"Holder- pretty boy! Holder- pretty boy!" Now

everyone is getting a chuckle at my expense.

"Aww even Donut likes that nickname," Ayida says while petting the "he who must not be named" looking creature.

"Let's get going! No reason to be wasting time!" I can't handle any more fun with these assholes.

It's getting late in the night when we finally pull into the warehouse parking lot. All of us shoved into Fletcher's SUV. *My dream come true...not.* Cole and Clint whispering about all the dirty things they did with Ayida before I got there. My dick couldn't have got any harder. And of course, Fletcher would notice me adjusting myself after climbing into the cramped space.

"What was y'all talking about back there?

Maybe how Blue took all three of our cocks at the same time today?" That conniving bastard.

"Nope, just talking plans. Y'all can wait inside. I'm going to be up there." I instruct while pointing at the small balcony on the second floor of the warehouse. "It's the perfect lookout for anyone coming towards us. If I see something, I'll message Clint. They have been breaking the door handle and coming in just to fuck stuff up. They figured out the first night that this isn't where we keep the good stuff. Y'all make sure guns are ready and watch your six. As soon as they open that door-"

"We know. This isn't our first rodeo, remember? When they open the door, we draw our guns and hold them. After everyone is situated, we'll decide to move them to the cabin or call the Family. We got it. Thank you." Clint says interrupting my lecture.

"Just don't be down here grab-assing, listen for my text. Don't get distracted." Everyone rolls their eyes, but nods anyway. I make my way to my post for the night and try to get comfortable. The last few times it was around midnight before anyone showed up, but I don't want to take the chance of missing them.

Taking out my night vision binoculars I take a glance at our surroundings. Unlike our other heavily fortified warehouse, this one is surrounded by other old buildings and parking lots. Nothing too interesting. The real treasure chests are out in the middle of nowhere. Beautiful land for miles around. Nobody would suspect to look where it is. It houses guns, drugs, and counterfeit money. Really a little of everything. This crap pile is just old paperwork, chop-shop car parts, and other bullshit that no one would really want. But I guess these guys didn't have any other way to get our attention without getting killed right away-so I reckon fucking up our shit was on the menu for the day.

Thirty minutes goes by fairly quickly. Only a few birds making sounds here and there as the frog's croak and lightening bugs flitter around. My phone gives out a silent hum suddenly and I'm on high alert. Waiting for the text to pop up on my screen, I hear the warehouse door creak open slowly. I focus my binoculars down, but instead of someone breaking in, someone is coming out. Fuck don't they realize they could mess this all up? If anyone sees them, they'll turn tail and run. I glance back at my phone and see a message from Clint.

"Has Ayida come up there yet? She said she needed to talk with you."

What could she want to talk about at this fucking moment? That girl really doesn't understand anything about this life. How could the guys be so stupid to let her come up here? Does she really have them that much under her control? Pussy-whipped bastards.

Looking back down to the door, I see her ponytail flapping in the wind. The humid summer weather feels pretty decent right now with the strong breeze blowing. My anxiety about talking to her outweighs my anger. I'm surprised by the somewhat happiness I feel at the chance for another conversation with the blue haired tyrant.

Then, a strange muffled sound pulls my attention back towards the ground. What the hell? Raising my binoculars, what I see has my heart in my throat and red fury filling my brain.

Chapter Twenty-Six: Ayida

Well, the guys have done it now. Thirty minutes straight of talking about how "Holder has a thing for you but he's too scared to say anything, and he needs someone like you in his life," and the best "We could all be together- a big family." I couldn't stand it another second. My belly was nothing but knots wondering if he really felt that way. I thought Holder was gorgeous from day one, but a major asshole in equal part. Turns out he is dealing with "daddy issues". He was truly scared of having to face his father's wrath if he let him down. He is messed up, but hell aren't we all? I told the guys I would go right up and have a quick chat and be right back down.

Standing outside the warehouse, I fix my ponytail and put "the girls" back in place. I feel like a badass in my combat boots, tight black jeans, and a black cropped t-shirt on. It was the best I had for this stealthy mission, and bonus points that I look pretty damn good too. It took me a while to get back my confidence after everything Robert took from me. My men have shown me what real love is. They know my weaknesses and flaws and have never taken advantage of or judged me for them. Now, I know only small minded *and small dick* men put others down to build themselves up. These Sons of Fortune have made me stronger and shown me my worth.

I won't ever let anyone put me down again.

Strutting my stuff to the side of the building where the steps start, I feel surprisingly good about the conversation I'm about to have with Hold. The sound of gravel crunching behind me and a feeling of dread overtakes me. Before I can turn around a thick dirty hand slams down over my mouth and another one around my waist. I'm being dragged backwards.

How did anyone sneak up with Holder as lookout? I can't even scream for any of them. I can feel the fear trying to sneak up into my throat, but I push it back down and let my rage grow in its place. I try to dig my heels into the dirt but can't gain purchase. I see more bodies quietly sneaking towards the warehouse as I'm hauled to the old building next door.

When my kidnapper finally leans down to whisper in my ear, I feel my anger bubble over. "You really thought five hundred miles would keep me away? That's pathetic-you're pathetic. "He spits out. "You are even more stupid than I thought. You'll never get away from me." The stench of his cheap cologne mixed with his old beef jerky breath makes me want to vomit. Fuck. Robert.

"What did you do to your fucking hair? We're gonna have to shave that off when we get back. Can't have you looking like a whore. People will talk. Ha, but I know the truth though. No one would have sex with you if they knew how stuck up you are. Just laying there like your dead. Frigid bitch. No wonder I had to go get my dick wet somewhere else." He laughs in my face, spittle across my cheek, before dropping me like a ton of bricks.

It's dark in the old building, but I can still see his sadistic eyes glinting at me. How did I ever have feelings for this turd-nugget? The only feelings I have now, looking at his ugly face, is bloodlust.

Standing up and brushing myself off I know without a shadow of a doubt that I want to piss him the fuck off before I kill him. I crack my neck and roll my shoulders. This is gonna be fun.

"It's funny you say that. I just had three guys fucking every hole I got, and I wasn't just lying there. I was screaming for more- *begging for it*. Maybe it was that tiny limp dick of yours that had me feeling dead, what with me trying not to laugh at it flopping around and all. Of course, maybe it was your shit ass breath in my face or hell it could be that kicked-in-the-head dumbass personality you have that turned me off. You are so fucking stupid you narcissistic asshole. I'm surprised you could even find my pussy, and when you did it was all over and done within one minute flat anyway."

I finish grinning like I just took first prize. I don't

know if I've ever felt better. Well except for when three amazing guys professed their love for me.

"Why you ugly, ungrateful fucking cunt! Who the fuck do you think you are talking to me like that? Your daddy ain't gonna save you. Those fuckboys you were with are already dead. I know you're lying anyway. Nobody would fuck you by choice!" He growls stalking towards me. I love this.

"Well why don't you come do something about it you ugly son of a bitch? Or are you too scared now that I beat your ass with a pole? I don't have one now. Don't be scared." I taunt shamelessly. He is positively seething. I swear I can see his body shaking.

"You goddamn bitch! I was gonna take you

home, punish you and then let you make it up to me, but you don't deserve mercy. I'm gonna strangle you and watch the life drain from your eyes!" He screams as he lunges for me.

My defense training with Old Man's trainer plus my offensive training in the gym with the guys kicks in; I side step him quickly and push my palm into the middle of his back sending him face first into the dusty floor with a thud.

"Gotta be quicker than that, pussy!" I cackle as I skip to the other side of the room.

I see what I'm going to use to finish this period in my life, leaning against a cabinet. I want to play with my prey a little longer though.

"Ahhh!" he screams again running at me with

his shoulder down like he means to tackle me. Stupid man. I sidestep again, but this time my palm lands on the back of his head pushing his face into the concrete floor. He lets out a pained cry. I'm sure that one broke his nose. I guess I need to finish this so I can check on my guys.

"Ya know Robert, I almost feel bad for you. *Almost.* I don't know what happened to you as a kid to make you so fucked up that you like to torture young girls to the point they would rather kill themselves than to live another day, but I just don't care anymore. You made my life hell, but now I know what heaven feels like, and I don't mean being loved and fucked by three beautiful men. That's just icing on this cake. I mean getting to beat the living shit out of you till you beg for death, and then beat you some more. I'm going to be the one to watch the life drain from YOUR eyes. Well, that is if there is anything left of them when I'm done." I taunt shrugging my shoulders.

Walking back to the pathetic blob on the floor, with the crowbar in my hand, I know this is the life I want. I want to be the hand of vengeance. If I'm going to touch the darkness, by God I will bend it to my will. I want to reap bloody pain on every woman and child beater and rapist. I want them to look at me with fear in their eyes as I stand over them and they see death herself. I want to be the last thing they see before their journey to hell to rot forever.

"Anything left to say, Robert?" I ask as politely as possible as I rear back my weapon of justice.

"Fuck you! You crazy bitch!" Ever the poet... Of course, he would make this easy for me.

"Bye Robert." I deadpan. Then I swing with every bit of strength I have in my body. The feeling of metal hitting bone sends vibrations up my arms. I pull back and swing again, but this time it's softer. I watch as blood pours from his open head wound and I feel nothing but excitement. It's a complicated feeling, but I crave it. I swing two more times before I turn the crowbar around and use it like a golf club.

"Fore!" I holler, making myself giggle. I swing again, this time my weapon is lodged in his temple behind his eye causing it to bulge out. There ain't no coming back, for Robert, from this anyway. His brain matter and blood are splattered over the floors and walls as well as coating me from head to toe.

I always said I would bathe in his blood and look at me now. I made it. He somehow still has something resembling a breath. I pound a few more times at his neck until I hear the crunch of his spinal column. That's better. I try to stop, but my body is on autopilot as I swing again and again. I don't stop until a hand grabs my wrist and pulls me to a hard body.

"Shhh you did it, Ayida. He's gone. You finished it. You can stop now." The surprise from hearing Holder's voice breaks me out of my trance.

"I did it. I did it. He's gone. It's done."

Chapter Twenty-Seven: Holder

Fuck! That was some shit. I was rushing to get to Ayida after I saw that creep grab her, but I got caught up with three other roided out goons. Finally, I made it to the building he had dragged her to. I was crouched down outside the broken window planning my next move when she started taunting and berating him. I almost laughed a few times but didn't want to blow my cover.

When he tried to attack her my first instinct was to jump in to save her, but she gracefully handled him. The idiot got slammed to the ground when he tried again. What I never would have expected was her grabbing a crowbar and going full on Joker on him. It was pretty damn amazing. I didn't realize what she had meant from her earlier statement, but she really does know how to lose control. By the time I made my way over to her there was blood and tissue covering the floor and most of her. After stopping her manic swings, I wrapped my arm around her shoulders to lead her back to the warehouse.

I will call the cleanup crew to deal with what is left of Robert. "You did good Blue. I'm proud of you." I don't have a chance to say anymore.

"Ayida! Ayida! Is she okay? Please tell me that's not all her blood!" Clint reaches us first. Scooping her up into his arms and squeezing, he nuzzles her blood-stained face. "I thought we lost you. I was so stupid! I should have never let you walk out of that door. I didn't think anyone would get to you with Holder right above us. Are you okay? I'm so sorry." Of course, he would be the one trying to take the blame. It's all our faults really.

"I don't know how they snuck up on me. I didn't hear or see a thing until they were on top of us. It's not just your fault. I was supposed to see them coming and somehow, I missed everything. I'm sorry to y'all and to Ayida." Wiping my face to find more blood splatter. She was swinging harder than I first thought. Even covered in blood she is stunning. Only my own freak brain would think that.

"Y'all stop being sorry. I shouldn't have gone outside, but I'm beyond happy I did."

"Is everyone okay? Whose blood is that and why is there so much?" Fletcher looks a little green as he and Cole are jogging towards us.

"It's Robert's." She answers gleaning with pride. Yep we are a lot more alike that I originally thought.

"So, he's?" Clint tries to ask while bobbing his shoulders.

"Dead. Finally, dead! This blood? It's all his!"

The guys just nod and look at me like I can answer an unknown question. Shrugging my shoulders, I make my way toward the SUV to make some phone calls.

This mess ain't gonna clean itself.

Chapter Twenty-Eight: Ayida

I can hear the blood pumping in my ears. My heart is racing. I feel high, but a different kind of high. A power high from taking the life of the person that made my life hell. Watching Holder stroll off with Robert's blood still fresh on him does something to my insides. I don't know why, but wetness starts building up between my thighs.

"I think I need to talk with Holder. I never got to say what I was going to earlier." Interrupting the guys' conversation. All heads turn in my direction.

"You want to talk about that now? Here? You don't want to get a shower and something to eat first?" Cole flinches with his questions. Geez. Overprotective alpha males.

"I know what I want and what I need. Thank y'all for looking out for me, but I can handle this." I say ending any argument they might have. Before I can turn to go find Holder, Fletcher puts his hand on my arm stopping my pursuit and pulling me off to the side.

"There's something you need to know before

you go waltzing into this situation. Holder might be big, bad, and blood loving', but he also has his hang ups. He has gone through a lot of bad shit in his life, and cause of that he always has to be in control and take care of everyone now. So, I'm gonna let you in on a secret... The one thing that he doesn't like controlling is sex. If you plan on doing what I think you're gonna do, you need to know he won't initiate anything. He won't take advantage of you or do anything you don't want. If anything, it will have to be you to take control. He just doesn't do well with that pressure on him. Ya catch my drift, Blue?"

I know I'm looking at him like a deer in headlights, slow blinking and all. My mind is trying to wrap around everything he is saying. "Are you saying... I get to be the one in charge. Like he'll do what I say? Are you pranking me, so I end up getting my ass spanked?" Holder looks like the type to smack my ass not the other way around.

Fletcher raises an eyebrow at me grumbling, "Mmmm. I want to spank your ass, but yes that's what I'm saying. He likes to be dominated. I'm not joking. I want y'all to get along and maybe make something of this. We love you Ayida and we love Holder. Y'all are important to us and we want y'all to be happy. If this makes y'all happy then even better," he says while patting my head.

"Sorry Blue. I love you, but I haven't got blood on these clothes yet. I would rather not do it by giving you a hug before you go fuck one of my best friends. Also remember the whole dominant thing only applies to him. Don't come back home thinking you're the boss," he laughs as I slap his arm.

"You're an ass, Fletch, but I still love you."

Walking towards the area I last saw Holder; I feel my nerves bundling up in my stomach. I've only ever listened to someone else "in the bedroom". How am I gonna tell someone what to do without getting flustered? I've almost talked myself out of everything when I see him standing next to Fletcher's SUV.

Holder is still splattered with blood and yelling into his phone. Fuck me, this Adonis looks so handsome in his rawness.

"Get here now or your ass is mine! I need this mess cleaned up before anyone calls the heads. If I have to call again, you'll be the one getting cleaned up from the floor." He ends the call throwing his phone into the SUV. Running his hand through his hair, it's easy to see the tension in his shoulders.

I'm beginning to grasp why he needs to be in control all of the time. If you're not in control, bad things can happen. Combine that with his killing tendencies and his parental issues... I can see how he would like to be out of control and dominated through sex. He needs someone confident so that he can enjoy himself and relax.

I'm not against the idea of being in control. Especially being in control of a man like Holder. Just the idea is getting me aroused again. The roaring sound is back in my ears as I look down at my blood-soaked clothes and imagine ordering him to undress me. The power high comes back quickly. I want to dominate Holder, but I also want to take care of him. If being controlled is what he needs, then I'm going to give him that. Challenge accepted.

Straightening my back, I stride towards him with purpose. Bringing his head up, he gives me a curious look. "What's up, Ayida? You okay?" Still worrying about me, but not for much longer. Bless his little black heart.

"Get in the SUV." I do my best to sound forceful.

"Excuse me?" He looks a little shocked.

"Get in the fucking SUV. I didn't say it was okay to ask questions."

"Did the guys tell you to do this? You don't have to do this Ayida. We're good as friends. I don't need to bring you into my fucked-up head after everything you've been through." He says looking at his feet. The change in his personality is instant. Like a completely different person. He is ashamed of his needs. I've been there and it's not a good feeling.

"Get in that fucking car now, Holder. Back seat. Floorboard. On your knees." His eyes shift up to mine as he gives a barely perceivable nod. Watching him open the back door and scoot in has my power high coming back full force. It is a major turn on to have a powerful man, a certified killer, do what I say. I slide in on the cool leather bench seat facing him. It's a tight fit, but it'll do.

I can feel his eyes roaming my body. Leaning in, I lick a line of blood from his cut cheek. When I pull back his eyes are wide with shock and arousal. "You're not the only one with bloodlust, Holder."

Grabbing his messy, blood soaked, blond hair, I crush my mouth to his. Pulling him closer, I run my tongue against his lips, but he doesn't allow me access. He wants to play this game.

Using his hair as leverage, I angle his head to the side and wrap my hand around his throat. Well, what I can grab. Holder isn't a small man. His eyes slide to mine, and the doubt is unmistakable. "If you really don't want me, I'll get out right now and we'll go back to the way it was. Friends only. If you're just unsure because of the guys, they have already given their blessings. If it's the fact that this is your kink and you're embarrassed, don't be, I want to dominate you. I want to choke you while I ride your cock. I want to make you clean my pussy with your tongue while your pearly white cum is dripping out of me. I'll take care of you. No matter what. This is your choice. Don't overthink it. Do you want me to get out?"

I wait while he takes in my words. My cunt already wet in anticipation. After a hard shake of his head, I dive back into his mouth with my hand tightening around his throat. This time there is no resistance- no hesitation.

Running one hand to his face to lightly slap him, I gauge his reaction. His little panting moan is all the encouragement I need. Leaning back in the seat and dragging him with me I get comfortable. "Undress me."

His fingers find the edge of my shirt and lift. He starts to reach for my black lacy bra. "Leave it." I command swatting his hand. Dragging my pants off my hips, his eyes widen, and his mouth opens. "Have you been dreaming of fucking my tight little pussy? How many times have you jacked off thinking of me riding your cock?"

His Adam's apple bobs as he swallows. "Tell me Holder. Now." I order.

"Every single fucking day. At least 3 times a day. I dream of licking up all your cum. Smelling you all day after you have ridden my face until you're sated.

Being tied to my bed and you using a crop on my thighs. Bite marks and bruises littering my body. I want everything you can give. Please."

I didn't know how much I would like this until right now. I would never really hurt him, but a little pain never killed anyone. "You want my handprints on you? My teeth digging in?" He nods slowly. "Then ask the right way."

"Please. Please hurt me." Fuck. Holder needs this. He probably doesn't even realize yet how badly. Grabbing his hair, I slap him across the face hard, and push him until his mouth is above my panty covered pussy.

"Stick your tongue out. I'm gonna use you as my own personal fuck-toy." Giving him what he wishes,

I rub my dripping cunt over his tongue and face. His hair still in one hand, I use the other to grab his neck and pull him even closer. Scratching down his neck and back leaving blood droplets in my wake. His moans against my pussy are almost enough to make me orgasm.

Pulling my panties to the side I use his tongue, grinding into it. Fucking myself with the tip and then rubbing it back over my sensitive nub. It's not long before I feel the familiar tingle, so I push his face flush to my pussy lips holding him in place to smother him in my cunt till I cum. Christ on a cracker, I'm cumming so hard on his tongue my body is spasming. My wetness coating his face and my juices dripping off his chin.

"Undress yourself. You're going to be my good boy, ain't you?" He nods while ripping his shirt off. His skin is damp with sweat and I can't help but lean over and lick around his nipple. He shudders but continues his task. Awkwardly removing his pants, I can see his hard cock straining against his boxers.

When he starts to slip them over his muscular ass, my mouth goes dry. His trouser snake springing free has my pussy dripping like a leaky faucet. Fuck me, his cock is long, thick, and studded with metal barbell piercings on the underside of his shaft with a ring piercing towards his head. "Sit with your hands underneath you. No touching. This is for me." He follows my order without hesitation.

Just seeing him sitting there, hands under his

ass, cock hard and laying against his toned stomach is driving me insane. Quickly, I slip my panties and bra off. Climbing on top of him, I grab his cock and tease myself with the head. Rubbing it around my clit and back to my tight ass, before dipping the tip into my core. He doesn't move, but his eyes close and his teeth dig into his bottom lip.

"Does my pussy feel good? Are you gonna let me ride that pierced cock hard for my pleasure? Do you want to feel my tight little cunt wrapped around your cock draining your balls dry?" I tease as I pull back and rub it over my clit again.

"Yes. Please fuck me. Please, I need your pussy." He whispers his plea as if a prayer or maybe a curse. His body tenses under me when I slide his cock in half-way.

"Do you deserve it?" I ask as I slide my bloody hands down his chest leaving handprints. There was something so fucking hot about Robert's blood on Holder. Just thinking back to ending the piece of shit and his blood showering over me has my libido in overdrive.

"Did you enjoy watching me kill that scum tonight? Did you get hard watching me covered in his blood? Are you like me, Holder? Do you crave the power of killing the evil in this world? Will you help me bring bloody justice to all of them?"

His eyes shoot open and look into mine. I know what he is feeling because I'm feeling the same thing. Acceptance.

"Yes. I don't need the power- the money- I NEED you. I'll torture and slaughter in your name. Just give the word." His answer has me driving myself down hard on his cock. He sucks in a breath between clenched teeth as I start to work myself faster and faster, chasing my release using his rod.

Grabbing his hair, I pull his head back to gain access to his throat. I run my tongue over his pulse before biting down into his salty skin. His hips jerk up to meet my fast rhythm. I savor the copper and salt taste on my tongue and let it drive me closer to an earth-shattering orgasm. The head of his cock rubbing the sensitive spot inside of my core has me right on the edge.

"Open your mouth and stick out your tongue."

When he complies, I rub my hard nipple over his warm tongue. "Suck on my nipples until you feel my cum dripping down your legs." Wrapping his lips around my pierced bud and sucking it into his mouth has me bouncing on his cock even harder. Chasing my orgasm. Damn it, his cock is a work of art and he has mastered his artform.

The little silver balls from his piercings rub my insides sending shivers up my spine. I brace my hands on his muscular shoulders and let my fingernails dig in- marking him- owning him. He moans around my nipple and the vibration sends shocks to my dripping cunt. I reach down and caress his balls feeling them lift and tighten as his moaning gets louder.

I'm right on the edge. I can feel the pressure building. "Please, mistress, put your hand over my mouth." Holder groans from under me. His eyes pleading. He is close too. Bringing my hand to his face I cover his mouth and press down. I steady myself with my other hand on the window leaving a bloody handprint smeared on the glass.

His hips jump up to meet me and I grind down even harder. His eyes locked with mine. I can feel his cock starting to pulse as his thrusting gets more erratic. The head swelling and massaging my g-spot is the last thing I feel before the world turns white behind my eyelids. My pussy clenches around his thick cock. His cum, hot and thick coats my walls. His moans turn to grunts and growls like a wild animal underneath me. Fuck, the mix of our fluids pooling between my thighs makes me squirm.

Taking my hand off his mouth, I'm not sure what to do. Does the whole Domme thing end when he finishes, or does it keep going? I'll do whatever he needs. Luckily, it doesn't take long to figure out what happens next when he grabs my face and kisses me so hard, I'm going to bruise.

"Thank you Ayida. Thank you for understanding me and not judging my kinks and hang ups. You are incredible. You still have some learning to do, but I'm excited to show you. You were so fucking sexy. You blow my gottdamn mind. You were born to dominate. You were born to rule us all." He groans in my ear as he kisses a trail down my throat.

"I'm glad you feel that way... 'cause if I

remember right, you're supposed to be cleaning me up now." I say arching my eyebrow at him. He grins and rolls me over on my back. Spreading my leg and kneeling back on the floorboard, he licks the trail of cum up my thighs to the junction of my legs. Starting at the curve of my ass and working up to the top of my pussy. He licks and sucks every drop of our combined fluids. Spending plenty of time circling my clit and diving back into my core to lap up everything he can. It doesn't take long before I'm cumming on his face again.

I pull up on his hair to get him to focus back on my eyes and not my pussy lips. "If you don't stop now, this is going to be a continuous thing. You clean me until I cum again and then you have to start over." I scooch away from him with a wink.

"You've done good- for now."

Chapter Twenty-Nine: Clint

"What the fuck did y'all do to my car?" Fletcher is furious. It's hilarious.

"Shut up Fletcher. I'll pay to get it cleaned." Holder replies shaking his head and trying to hide his smirk.

Even with the SUV's tinted windows, you can see the bloody handprints and streaks. The inside smells like blood and sex. I'm fairly sure I saw a cum spot in the backseat. They definitely had a good time and left the evidence for everyone to see.

I'm getting hard just thinking about her naked body writhing in the seat behind me not even fifteen minutes ago. Holder and Blue were crawling out from the backdoor right when we were getting ready to leave. Her neat ponytail was now hanging down her back with stray hairs sticking out around her face. Her lips swollen and stained red with blood. Her shy smile hiding the savage woman we all saw earlier.

"So y'all work everything out? We all good

now?" I question, looking in the rearview mirror. It's already well after midnight and we are finally heading home. Well, my home. I guess it's turned into everyone's crash pad now. It's the only place big enough for all of us. I don't mind though. It's nice having a houseful of people I care about.

"Yes, we're good. I'm just ready to get a shower and a good night's sleep." Blue says around a yawn.

"She might be a stone-cold killer, but she's a cute killer. She's our little killer. "Holder says, slinging his arm behind Blue's shoulders pulling her close- drawn to her like a magnet.

"I'm still mad at y'all for doing me and my car dirty like this. Shit, I haven't even 'christened' it with Blue myself yet and you fucked that up for me. Y'all could have found a bathroom or something. Geez, I mean it looks like a bloody Picasso painting and the sex scene from the "Titanic" movie decided to have a baby in the backseat. Fuck my life," Fletch grouses.

Damn, he can be a whiny asshole sometimes. "Your ride will be fine, and you will too. Look at it this way, it's a good reason to get you a new one! Maybe something really 'fancy' with bullet proof glass and an easy to clean interior?" I can't help but chuckle at his horror-stricken face. I guess he really is attached to the big bulky thing.

"How can you even joke like that? This baby has got us to many jobs and parties. It's basically part of the family. They had sex inside a family member!

You deviants!" He yells with as much enthusiasm as possible while looking at them in the rearview mirror.

Holder's smiling face and the sound of metal hitting metal is the last I see and hear before my world turns black.

"What the hell was that? Is everyone alright?" Cole's voice sounds muffled to my ringing ears. My head hurts too bad to open my eyes. I feel around me trying to orient myself with my surroundings. I can tell right away the SUV is on its side. My first guess being we were hit from the side; that explains how Fletcher and I didn't see it coming.

"Blue? You okay?" Holder's soft words reach my ears and my heart rate kicks up a notch. Prying my eyes open, I try to turn around towards the backseat. My whole body aching in response. "Blue? Blue? Where is she?" Holder's panic palpable.

"Ugh! What the fuck happened? Why is everyone screaming?" Fletcher asks, finally drawing my attention to him. Blood is trickling down his face from a small wound on his forehead. Otherwise he looks fine. He has definitely looked a lot worse before.

"Blue is missing! Everyone out of the car! We have to look for her. She might have gotten thrown out!" Cole's voice verging on hysterical comes from the very back. Unbuckling, I help Fletcher crawl out of his shattered window first before following him out. Meeting with the other guys in the front.

"Ayida? Blue? Come on Blue. Say something!" Cole and Holder call while sweeping the nearby roadside. Fletcher is still standing by the flipped SUV staring at it in shock and rubbing the nap of his neck. My mind finally catching up with my eyes I notice something is missing.

"Guys! Where's the other car? We were hit on the driver's side by something, but I don't see another car or people?"

"Fuck my life! We assumed it was just her ex getting help from someone to get her back. What if she was the target for someone else entirely from the start, and they were just using his dumbass to get to her? We let our guard down and we've lost her!" Holder screams while pacing back and forth and rubbing his chest like being away from Ayida is physically ripping his soul out.

He could be right about her being kidnapped. We've had rivals in the past, but everything has been quiet for years until now. You don't get to be as powerful as the Saupoudrer Family without pissing some people off along the way. I'm still not sold though. No one even knew Ayida was back, but the Family, and she hasn't even met the other heads yet.

"Someone call Bastien! We need a ride now. Every minute we waste someone could be hurting her." Fletcher orders with an authoritative voice I have never heard from him before. A mixture of grief and rage evident with every word. He is right, even if it's not one of our rivals, whoever took her didn't have anything good in mind.

"Call Old Man. We're gonna need his help."

Chapter Thirty: Ayida

Damn my head is pounding. What the fuck happened? One minute we were all laughing and picking on Fletcher and the next- blackness. I try to open my eyes, but they are gritty and burn. I can hear voices, but none are familiar. Swallowing, my throat feels like I've eaten glass.

"Ahh, the whore is finally awake. Took you long

enough, cunt," a thick southern voice mocks from behind me. Finally coming all the way back to reality, I realize I'm lying on cold concrete with my hands and feet tied. This is just fucking perfect, my gottdamn luck. I finally get my ultimate revenge on Robert only to be kidnapped by some asshole I don't even know.

"Who the hell are you and what do you want with me?" I grumble while trying to get into a sitting position. It's hard to be taken seriously when you're laying face first on the ground.

"You don't know me, but Robert did. You could say we're old friends from back in Tennessee. He was supposed to be collecting you for me as payment for all the money he owed. As you know, the man had a bad drug problem and no job. He told me about the bitch that beat him and ran like a coward. How her dad was a head for a big crime family down south and that her daddy would pay anything, give anything, for his little girl. So, we made a deal." I can hear the glee in his voice even without seeing his surely sadistic smile.

"You in exchange for his debt being paid in full, and he could walk away bullet holes free. Would have been a sweet deal for him, if you wouldn't have bashed his skull in like a pinata. Was still pretty fun to watch though. I'd give it a solid 9 out of 10 for your effort. But alas, I couldn't let an opportunity like this get away... You can call me Chuck." The voice finishes as I finally tear my eyes open.

A middle aged, balding man with wrinkled khakis and a golf polo shirt- collar popped and all is standing above me. His image is a letdown. I was imagining a big, muscled up, prison tatted, maybe throw in some vicious scars from previous fights looking gangster. This guy could be someone's creepy uncle. Ugh, I'm gonna have to kill creepy "Uncle" Chuck. Only I would get kidnapped by a man with velcro orthopedic shoes.

"This here is Jimmy. He is the actual person responsible for your abduction and will handle your ransom. He was my other way in, you know, in case something happened to poor Robert. Jimmy here has worked with the Saupoudrer Family for a while. He was all too happy to help me out for a pay raise. Them Sons you were fucking sure are stingy." Chuck says, turning his back to me.

"Speaking of fucking, Jimmy here had a second request if you catch my drift. Seems you have a secret admirer Miss Underhill. So, I'll be leaving him to it. You're not exactly my type. Y'all kids have fun!" He calls while leaving the little concrete room through a steel door.

This second gangly man draws my attention. Tall and skinny with a pockmarked face and yellow teeth. Jimmy is slightly more intimidating than creepy "Uncle" Chuck, but still underwhelming. "I have been tortured and raped before. It'll take a lot more to scare me!" I say, raising my voice strong and clear.

"That's fine. I would rather you be scared, pussy

tightens up that way, but you can enjoy it too. Anything works for me. I'll probably have to use that asshole though since you've been whoring around with all them men. I can't wait for Fletcher to find out I screwed his precious little blue-haired beauty till she was leaking with my spunk." He cackles, his janky teeth on display.

I want to gag just thinking about him near me, but I refuse to show fear. I've come too far to let this nasty fuck have that kind of power over me. He might rape me, but it'll be him getting fucked with a crowbar when I get out of these restraints.

"Fletcher and the guys will want to kill you, but I won't let them. I'm gonna be the one to pluck out your eyes and feed them to my bird. So, come on over here. If you think you can handle me. I bet a thousand dollars your dick is smaller than Robert's and he was so small he needed two cock rings for me to feel it." I can't help but taunt him. I've learned a mad man is more likely to make mistakes than a calm one. So, if I can have fun and fuck his face up, might as well kill two birds with one stone.

"You pretentious little twat. You're going to be crying when I get done with you. No one to save you now." He grins as he stalks in my direction. I ready a plan in my head. Before I can get another word out, he grabs me by my shirt, ripping it open and exposing my bra, and flips me face down again. My heart kicks up a notch, but I refuse to let panic rule me.

Straddling the back of my thighs he leans in to whisper in my ear. "Not so chatty now, are you bitch? Do you feel my hard dick on your ass? I'm about to rip you apart with my cock." Licking my ear, I see my chance. Swinging my head back and to the side as hard as I can. I connect and hear a crunching sound.

"You really thought I would make it that easy for you? Try again slim. Your ugly ass is gonna have to fight for this pussy." Rolling over on my back, I can't control my laughter as blood spews from his nose that he is clutching. I recognize my second shot. Kicking with both legs straight up into his crotch, he lets out the highest pitched scream I have ever heard. I'm guessing dogs are howling somewhere in the distance.

"You fucking bitch! You're going to pay!" He screeches while falling on top of me. If he kills me now, it was still worth it. Breaking his nose and tiny pecker was almost as fun as slaughtering dear ole Robert. Jimmy's arm pulls back, and his fist connects with my cheek. Stars light up my eyelids as he continues his assault. He gets in four more blows before he is being pulled off of me. A punishing kick to the ribs is the last he gets in before Chuck escorts him from the room. Yup, definitely still worth it.

Waking up sorer than I've been in months is an unwelcome feeling. Memories flood back and my heart drops as realization dawns on me. I'm still laying on the concrete floor, and who knows how long I've been out. I strain to shake off my mental fog and remain awake. After roughly thirty more minutes, I hear the steel door open. I brace myself for more hits, but none come.

"Get up. Someone is here to see you." Chuck's southern drawl sounds more nervous than before. Sliding a hand under my arm he pulls me to standing and I crack one eye open. He leads me out of the room and up some old wooden stairs to a big auditorium. We're in my old high school. Looks like he was keeping me in the tornado shelter in the basement.

"Schatzi! You okay? What did you do to her? Her face is black and blue, and her clothes are torn!" Old Man's voice is angry and dark. What is he doing here? Why did they bring him here? He might be mean and a badass, but he is too old for this crap.

He may be a mafia leader but he's MY dad.

"She'll be fine as long as y'all brought what y'all said. Tell where it is and then I'll hand her over." Comes Jimmy's nasally voice. I guess I did break his nose. Good. Serves the bastard right. When I get done with him, a broken nose will be the least of his problems. Struggling to keep my swelling eyes open, I finally see my guys. Standing behind Old Man with big metal chests between them and guns hanging from their shoulder holsters. They are bruised and battered almost as bad as me. Just another reason to fuck Jimmy's world up.

"You okay, Blue? Did they do anything to you?" Fletcher's voice rings out in the old auditorium. Jimmy is holding me by my shirt in front of him, like his own personal shield, and I can't see behind me.

"She is fine. Y'all bring those trunks over here and open them for us to see. If everything looks good, we'll let her walk back with her dear old Dad." Chuck says from behind me, but I don't trust him or Jimmy as far as I can throw them. I know slimy, Chuck and Jimmy could out slide a slug.

"Hell no! You send her over and we'll leave." Old Man orders sounding every bit as authoritative as he did when I was a kid. He does not do well with bullies, and that's all these two pricks are.

"No can do, Old Man. How about this... We'll walk over there with the princess, check the goods, and y'all can leave? Sound good to y'all?" Jimmy asks without even looking in Fletcher's direction.

"Yeah that'll work. Hurry up though these idiots haven't had a bath yet and they are starting to get ripe. Especially this one." Old Man says while nodding his head in Holder's vicinity.

Said "stinky man's" face is priceless. "What the hell, Old Man?"

Dragging me down the aisle between the bleachers, I can't help but to remember all the talent shows and plays that went on here. I despised high school bullshit, and I had no friends here. To think I could have died underneath the place I hated the most growing up makes me shudder. Thank God for small favors. Getting to the end of the aisle, Chuck passes us to meet Old Man at the first trunk.

"Looks good. Y'all open the rest and step back."

He orders while walking towards the other trunks. Taking his time to look over bricks of weed and a cache of weapons that I've never seen before, he finally turns to Jimmy and me. "Cut her loose. She is free to go." He commands the ugly fucker still holding me by the back of my shirt.

I feel the steel of his knife against my wrist as he silently cuts my restraints. Then he shoves me with a hand to the middle of my back sending my sprawling on to the floor.

"You fugly rat bastard." I mumble under my breath. When I get out of this, and he doesn't have guns all around him, I'm going to end his worthless life. It may just be him and Chuck out here, but I can almost guarantee some more hired thugs are around here somewhere just waiting to finish us off.

"Come on Schatzi. Let's go home." Old Man's voice calls to me. Keeping me from turning around and doing something stupid. Dragging myself to my feet, I shuffle towards Old Man and the guys. They keep glancing at me worriedly, and then back to glaring at the men behind me. I can't wait to just be back in their arms. When I finally make it to the group of men, Old Man is the first to wrap his arms around me.

"I can't handle another day like this. Thinking of almost losing you was like losing your momma all over again. My poor heart can't handle that." I take the time to memorize the smell of menthol and coffee rolling off of him. When he's anxious he smokes like a chimney and needs a cup of coffee for each cig. It's a comforting smell after everything that's happened.

It doesn't take long for the guys to surround me after Old Man finally releases his tight hold. "Are you okay? Did they hurt you?" Cole asks tentatively. While hugging me close.

"We'll kill them anyway." Holder growls when it's his turn to tuck me under his chin.

"Do you need a doctor?" Of course, Clint would be the logical one. While my poor normally happy-go-lucky Fletcher looks lost for words. He just jerks me tight to his body and holds me with his cheek resting on top of my head.

"I'm so sorry. I didn't see them. If I would have had my eyes on the road..." A tearful break in Fletcher's voice. I don't let him finish.

"It doesn't matter. They would have waited till I was alone. They were determined to get me anyway they could. This is not any of Y'all's fault. Let's just get home so I can shower and then come up with a plan to destroy them."

With Old Man on one side and my guys on the other, we start towards the double doors leading out of the auditorium. Then I hear it. The click of a rack sliding into place. Before I can even turn around, I hear the shots ring out. All I can do is brace myself as something heavy hits me in the back knocking me to the floor.

Landing on my left cheek, the guys are in my view. All of them sprawled on the ground. My heart is beating out of my chest. They are yelling at me, but I can't hear from the blood pumping in my ears. I'm also pinned to the floor so I can't get up. Was I shot? Is this what it feels like?

Almost like it was never there, the weight is removed, and I roll to my side. My heart shatters into a million pieces. Old Man, is laying next to me, clutching his chest. His normally starched and pressed button up is soaked in thick red oozing blood. I feel nauseous. This has to be a nightmare. This can't be real. I close my eyes demanding to wake up. Only to open them to the same horrible scene.

Crawling over to him, I lay my head on his barely moving chest. "Hold on Old Man. I'll get help. The guys will do something. Just hold on." I beg, but I've seen people die before and know the glassy look of his eyes.

"Schatzi, it'll be okay. You're not alone anymore. You have the Sons and you'll be okay. I need to tell you something. Please listen for once." His voice just above a whisper. "You are my whole world. Before you it was your momma. Schatzi, I don't think your momma died like we thought. I think someone wanted her gone. I have a folder..." His words are just jumbled nonsense I can't make sense out of. "Up... to you now. I... love...you." The last words I can understand before a sigh escapes his pale lips.

"Old Man? Wake up! Wake up! Daddy! Please wake up!" I press my ear to his warm sticky chest, but I can't hear anything. He's gone. I finally have a relationship with him, and someone ripped him from me. They will die today. Sitting up and looking around, I finally notice what's going on around me. At least ten goons have come out from hiding. Shooting towards our side of the auditorium. Holder is in front of me keeping them at bay. The other guys are ducked behind the seats, using them as cover, and then popping up to return fire.

"Ayida? Is he ... is he gone?" Holder asks over his shoulder. He can't turn around to see my grief.

"He's gone. Where's Chuck and Jimmy? Did you see who did it?" I ask while using my arm to rub some of Old Man's blood off my face. I more than likely just smeared it and look like a monster. That's fine though. I want Jimmy and Chuck to piss their pants when they see this monster coming for them.

"Jimmy was holding the gun. Chuck was screaming at him. My best guess is Jimmy was trying to take you out on his own." Holder replies to me. Doesn't matter. They both will die. If Chuck wouldn't have ever wanted to kidnap me this would never have happened. He is guilty by association.

"Cover me!" I yell at Holder and take off crouched as low as I can get.

It's time for me to hunt my prey.

I can hear his angry, "What the Fuck?" behind me before shots ring out and I'm deaf again. I make a straight path to the trunks the guys had brought in. Finding tactical rifles, handguns, knives and hand grenades.

Bloody brilliant. Things are about to get fun.

I load up with everything I can carry and make my way back to Holder. "Remember our conversation in the car? You are mine to command. Well, help me find Chuck and Jimmy. Don't shoot to kill. I want them to die slowly and painfully. Understand?"

Like a switch was flipped, his eyes turn cold and calculating. "Yes ma'am." He leads the way with me right behind him. Picking off the 2 stray goons in our vicinity, we make our way up to the stage curtain and through a set of doors leading to the very back.

I remember where this goes. We find the hallway that leads to the gym. Slowly creeping up to the doors I can hear Chuck's panicked voice.

"Why did you do that? We got what we wanted. Now the rest of the Family will send their entire syndicate after us! I'm screwed. I don't get my hands dirty. I'm the Boss. Why didn't you listen?" He cries to Jimmy.

As quietly as possible, Holder pushes the door open and we slide inside. Staying close to the wall we go unnoticed to the arguing idiots.

"Listen you pussy. They would have come after us no matter what. You can't kidnap the daughter of Frank Underhill and just walk away. Someone had to die. I prefer the fighting chance of taking them out first. Now, help me get this to the car!" Jimmy screams back at Chuck, making him jump to action moving one of the trunks towards the exit doors of the gym.

I can't stay quiet anymore. They have guns slung over their shoulder so now is the time to act. "Chuck, Chuck, Chuck…. Are you really going to take orders from this low-level gun runner? I thought you were 'the Boss'? I guess not anymore. Ya know- you didn't hit me, you didn't try to rape me, and you didn't make me an orphan, so I'll show you some mercy." I say sweetly with my tactical rifle trained on his back. "Y'all turn around slowly with your hands in the air. I want to remind y'all that two guns are pointed in Y'all's direction right now."

They both turn towards me not making any quick moves. At least they ain't that stupid. "Jimmy on the other hand... I'm going to rip his balls off and make him eat them, right before I pluck out his eyes for Donut- as Jimmy and I previously discussed." I say shrugging my shoulders. Before I can say anything else, Holder's rifle jumps next to me and Chuck falls to the ground right after.

"I thought you were going to show him mercy!" Jimmy's frantic voice screams at me.

"Do you see him eating his balls, Jimmy? No! I say that's mercy." I reply while stalking closer to him. I swear I can smell the stench of fear coming off him in waves.

"Look, I'll do anything. I can tell you all kinda

stuff. There is talk coming from the border... A new gang is coming up from Miami and they want this spot. This is the perfect place between Miami and Texas. If they can take over here, they can control the South East and South West. They are coming for the heads. I can be a mole. I can help y'all. You don't know anyone else with this advantage."

What he is saying is interesting, but nowhere close enough to keep me from tearing his face to shreds.

"Really interesting Jimmy, but sadly the only thing I want from you are your screams." I say calmly before aiming my rifle at his knee and firing. The sound he makes is pure bliss to my ears.

I wasn't always so happy to hurt someone. Evil

men turned me into this bloodthirsty monster. They only have themselves to blame. Robert started it the first time he hit me, Chuck did it when he kidnapped me, and Jimmy here was the nail in the coffin. Hurt me- you're going to die. Hurt the people I love? You're going to suffer first.

I feel Holder getting closer. "Hold, I know you enjoy this as much as I do, but I need this one. He is mine. You can have the next one." I say as I pat his cheek. I notice Old Man's blood is drying on my hands and it sets a bomb off in my chest. Stomping over to Jimmy's still screaming form, I shoot his other kneecap at point blank range.

"You haven't seen anything yet." I spit at him as I draw the serrated knife from my hip. Kneeling over his squirming body, I start to carve his face and chest. His screams like the most beautiful song I've ever heard.

I don't know how long I "play" with him before someone's hands are pulling me up from Jimmy's body. Arms wrapping me in a tight hug as I struggle to get free. The smell of cinnamon and leather brings me back to reality. Clint's sweet face framed by Cole and Fletcher's.

"It's okay, Blue. It's over we got you." Clint's soothing voice, like a balm to my raw nerves. His chest is covered in blood and I start to panic, but he quickly calms me. "Blue, that's not my blood. That came from you." Looking down I see I'm drenched again. I never even got to clean up from killing

Robert. I turn in his arms and find Holder checking Jimmy's pulse.

"He's gone. Lasted longer than I thought." He declares getting up from his kneeling position. I walk closer to inspect my handiwork. Apparently, I go full feral when I black out. You can't even make out Jimmy's face. Even his eyelids are gone. I'm simply happy to know he suffered before he took his last breath.

"Take me home. I'm filthy, tired, and really fucking hungry. I'm in the mood for pizza, a shower, a nap, and four cocks- not necessarily in that order…"

THE END

Epilogue

His casket is beautiful. The flowers are gorgeous. The service was perfect. Today is the day I say my final goodbyes to my Old Man.

"You okay, Blue? It's almost over." I know Cole is trying to make me feel better, but I don't want it to be over. When I leave here that means it's real.

Right now, it could still be a bad dream. A nightmare. I just want to wake up now.

"I'm fine, Cole. Just hug me, please." Giving me a small smile, he wraps his huge tattooed arms around my shoulders. It's not just him though. I feel Fletcher's arms around my waist. Clint and Holder's hands rubbing and soothing my legs.

"We all love you and are here for you, Blue." Comes Fletcher's voice muffled by my hair. I know he is telling the truth, and my heart flips again. Since that horrible night, the guys have treated me like a princess. Cooking for me, bathing me, holding me... They even took turns cleaning Donut's cage. Most of all they haven't ordered me to talk. They have just been supportive and let me grieve the way I needed.

They have entwined themselves in my heart irrevocably. That's real love.

Before his casket is lowered into the grave, I lay my yellow rose on top feeling sentimental. "Bye Old Man. Tell momma I love her and miss her. Y'all have fun until I get there, because then it's going to get wild." I whisper as a lean down to kiss the warm wood.

With tears streaming down my face, I walk hand in hand with Clint and Fletcher. My other guys flanking us. We are a unit- a family. Nothing can tear apart.

Reaching Fletcher's new SUV, a thin older man wearing an expensive suit stops us.

"Miss Underhill, you have been summoned.

Please, come with me." What the hell? Why would I go anywhere with a stranger?

"Umm, no thanks. Maybe another time," I reply noncommittally when Holder's hand wraps around my arm.

"Ayida, this is Jeffrey. He works for the heads. You need to go with him. We're not allowed in their meeting, but you'll be okay. No one will harm you there." He explains while I look back and forth between my men. They all nod their agreement. I guess I'm going.

They all kiss me gently and watch as Jeffrey slips his arm through mine to escort me to the long black town car waiting for us. He opens the rear door and I slide in. The leather is cool from the air conditioning, and it's a welcome relief from the humid Louisiana heat.

Getting in the driver's seat he turns to me, "Buckle up Miss Underhill. Safety first," he says with a friendly grin.

"Jeffrey, why am I being summoned? Can you at least tell me that much? It's been a long few day and I don't feel like playing games." I grumble. I'm also hungry so I'm not in the best mood.

Jeffrey peers at me through the rearview mirror and I can still see his happy expression.

"Well, I guess I can let you in on the little secret, Miss Underhill... I will be working for YOU very shortly."

Reborn In Blue

Next in Series:

Purgatory In Pink

Colors of Corruption, Book 2

-SNEAK PEEK-

Chapter One: Ayida

"Excuse me? Working for me?" My hindbrain

has a hard time keeping up with his words. What does that even mean?

"You look confused. Let me clarify. The Family is offering you Mr. Underhill's seat at the table. You'll be one of the heads. An equal part in the power that is the Saupoudrer Family." My driver Jeffrey explains with an even bigger grin.

I'm in complete shock. "Jeffrey, do they know I'm new to all the crime stuff? That I've only been learning from Old Man for a few months?" I question the sanity of this "Family". I mean the Sons of Fortune have years more experience than me. Any of them would be better candidates than me.

"Yes, Miss Underhill. They know that. They also know you beat a man to death with a crowbar for trying to hurt you again, and you also avenged your father by carving his killer's skin and muscle from his bones. You're not one to be taken lightly. If you don't want the position, it will just close. Mr. Underhill didn't have anyone else to take it. The other children have to wait until their fathers pass down the positions or they die." He says while turning on some old jazz music to play quietly. Effectively ending the conversation.

My mind starts to wonder. I've replayed Old Man's final words over and over in my head. He thought Momma was murdered. He wanted me to prove it. If I turn down this position, I will still have money, but I won't have power. In this world you need both. I won't ever find out anything if I'm not in the Family. The guys could help, but I need to do this myself. That solidifies my answer.

Pulling up to a huge old stone building, I notice that it resembles a gothic cathedral complete with lancet stained-glass windows, flying buttresses, and steepling at the roof. I take a deep steadying breath and a plan takes hold in my head. I'm not weak. I'm not helpless. I am a strong badass woman. Maybe I'm exactly what the Saupoudrer Family needs. Someone to shake things up.

Jeffery holds open the big arched door for me to enter. The inside is aesthetically pleasing. It's filled with elaborate tapestries, old paintings, and other medieval looking decor. It screams real "old money" people. Walking down the vaulted hallway I can hear voices at the end. Arguments if I had to guess. I imagine some of the heads probably don't want me here, but that's just too bad. I'm grabbing life by the balls, I'm here, and I'm about to get some shit done. I straighten my spine and get ready for battle.

"You watching this, Old Man? I'm doing what you taught me. Cause a little hell and have a lot of fun." I say to the ceiling.

Pushing through the double doors into what appears to be a surprisingly open and radiant boardroom, heads swing in my direction. I'm greeted with smiles and scowls. I spy my seat and walk with purpose to it. Sliding into the tall, leather, wingback chair I lace my fingers on top of the marble tabletop.

"I hear y'all have something to ask me?"

Soundtrack

1. Art of Dying, "Tearing Down the Wall" (Prologue)

2. Fleetwood Mac "Landslide" (Chapter 1)

3. Fall Out Boy, "Irresistible" ft. Demi Lovato (Chapter2)

4. Big Data, "Dangerous" ft. Joywave (Chapter 2)

5. The Corrs, "Breathless" (Chapter 3)

6. Frank Sinatra, "My Funny Valentine" (Chapter 4)

7. I Prevail, "Breaking Down" (Chapter 4)

8. Jace Everett, "Bad Things" (Chapter 5)

9. Earth, Wind & Fire, "September" (Chapter 9)

10. Michael Bublé, "Feeling Good (Chapter 14)

11. Muse, Madness" (Chapter 16)

12. Twenty-One Pilots, "My Blood" (Chapter 17)

13. Hank Williams," Jambalaya" (Chapter 21)

14. George Jones, "The Race is On" (Chapter 21)

15. Pixies, "Where is My Mind" (Chapter 25)

16. Led Zeppelin, "Trampled Under Foot (Chapter 26)

17. Anthrax, "The Devil You Know" (Chapter 29)

18. Talking Heads, "Psycho Killer" (Chapter 30)

19. Incubus, "Wish You Were Here" (Epilogue)

20. Doja Cat, "Boss Bitch" (Book 2, Chapter 1)

Reborn In Blue

About the Author

M.J. Knight is a self-confessed collector of tattoos, comic book figurines, and books. She lives with her husband and their five kids in Decatur, Alabama. She spends most days wrangling her kids, cooking, and binge watching "Grey's Anatomy"- but not necessarily in that order.

When she isn't busy with her everyday chaos, you will find her typing away about characters that she loves and relates to the most in hopes that her fans can live vicariously through their adventures.

If you want to know more about M.J.'s future books and projects- join her

Facebook group: Knights of Sin
Instagram: MJKnight_Author

Good Reads: M.J Knight

Amazon: M.J Knight

Where the talk is real, the memes are funny, and you might just find your next sinfully delicious book boyfriend!

Printed in Great Britain
by Amazon